THE SURVIVALIST 2
THE NIGHTMARE BEGINS

The Survivalist series by Jerry Ahern, published by New English Library:

1: TOTAL WAR
2: THE NIGHTMARE BEGINS
3: THE QUEST
4: THE DOOMSAYER
5: THE WEB
6: THE SAVAGE HORDE
7: THE PROPHET
8: THE END IS COMING

THE SURVIVALIST 2
THE NIGHTMARE BEGINS

Jerry Ahern

NEW ENGLISH LIBRARY

First published in the USA in 1981 by
Kensington Publishing Corporation

First NEL Paperback Edition May 1983
Reprinted June 1984
Reprinted November 1984
Reprinted August 1985

NEL Books are published by
New English Library,
Mill Road, Dunton Green,
Sevenoaks, Kent.

Editorial office: 47 Bedford Square, London WC1B 3DP

Printed and bound in Great Britain by
Cox & Wyman Ltd, Reading

British Library C.I.P.

Ahern, Jerry
The nightmare begins.—Survivalist; 2
I. Title II. Series
813'.54[F] PS3551.H/

ISBN 0-450-05574-4

For Sharon, Jason, and Samantha – who've survived a whole hell of a lot with me – love always.

Chapter One

General Ishmael Varakov buttoned the collar of his greatcoat and pulled the sealskin chopka down lower on his balding head. "Chicago—another Moscow," he muttered to himself, shivering, standing in the doorway of his helicopter and staring across the sea of mud at the icy, wind-tossed Lake Michigan waters beyond. "Bahh!" he grunted, starting down the rubber-treaded three steps leading to the damp ground. He stared at the massive edifice less than twenty-five yards distant. He didn't bother to look for the name—it had been the Museum of Natural History, given to the city of Chicago for a world's fair decades earlier and bearing the name of a capitalist, Varakov thought he recalled.

"Put up a new name," he said, turning to his young female aide, watching her legs a moment as the wind whipped at the hem of her skirt. "You are freezing—come—inside. But the new name I want should reflect that this is headquarters for the North American Army of Occupation of the Soviet Peoples'

Republic—make a note of this when your hands stop trembling with the wind."

He walked ahead, spurning the blotchy red carpet waiting for him between the ranks of Kalashnikov-armed, blustery-faced troops, crossing the mud instead, his mirror-shined jackboots sinking at times several inches into the mire under the mass of his two hundred eighty-five pounds.

He stopped, standing at the base of the long low steps, scraping the mud from the soles of his footgear and staring up at the building.

"Comrade General Varakov!"

Varakov turned, staring at the major standing at rigid attention on his left. Varakov returned the salute, less than formally and grunted, "What is it, major?"

"General! I have the seventeen partisans ready."

Varakov just stared at the major, then somewhere at the back of his mind he remembered the radio dispatch given him when he had landed at International Airport, northwest of the city, before transferring to his helicopter. He could recall it clearly enough—seventeen armed partisans had been captured after attacking one of the first Soviet scout patrols sent into the city. The seventeen—three of them women—had killed twelve Soviet soldiers. The partisans had survived the neutron radiation when Chicago was bombed, having taken refuge in an underground shelter. They had been armed with American sporting guns.

"I will come, major," Varakov nodded, then stopped scraping the mud from his boots—looking in the direction the major pointed, Varakov could see there was more mud. The major walked beside him, Varakov's young female aide a respectable distance behind. As Varakov stepped into the mud again, he silently wondered what it had been like here on the lakefront when the waters had so suddenly risen. The planetarium less than a quarter mile away had been badly damaged, the museum—now headquarters—barely touched. The brunt of the force of the Seiche that had swamped much of the city, destroying everything in its path like a tidal wave, had hit the northern shoreline. The houses and apartments of the rich capitalists had been there and were now in ruins. Varakov did not smile at the thought. The rich, too, had a right to life.

Varakov stared up from the mud, noticing the major had stopped. Looking ahead, Varakov saw the seventeen—some of them little more than children, none of them over twenty, he judged. He transferred his stare from the wall where they stood—hands bound, eyes blindfolded—and looked to the squad of six men, submachine guns in their gloved hands.

"Would you care to give the order to fire, comrade general?" the major asked.

"No—no, they are your prisoners." Then, stifling his own emotions, he added, "It is your honor."

The major beamed, executed a salute which Varakov—again less than formally—returned.

The major executed an about-face and walked to a position beside the firing squad. "Ready!"

"Aim!"

"Fire!"

Varakov did not turn away as the six-man squad began their steady stream of automatic fire, the seventeen Americans in front of the wall starting to crumple. One tried running, his eyes still blindfolded, hands still tied, and he fell face down into the mud as two of the soldiers fired at him at once. Varakov looked again. The one who had tried running had been a young girl, not a man. As the last body fell, Varakov stared at the wall—it was chipped with bullet pocks and there were a few dark stains—either from blood or from the mud that had splashed as the dead people had fallen.

Mechanically—still shivering—Varakov grunted, "Very good, comrade major," this time not saluting at all.

Chapter Two

Varakov wiggled his toes in his white boot socks under the massive leather-covered desk at the far end of the central hall. He looked up, for what must have been, he felt, the hundredth time, at the Egyptian murals on the upper walls. "Catherine," he grunted, looking across the room at the young aide rising from her desk and starting across the azure-blue carpet toward him. "Never mind walking here—order lights. This is too dark here. Go!"

She started a formal about-face and he waved her away, looking back to the reports littering his desk. Varakov glanced at the Swiss-movement watch on his left wrist and leaned back into his leather chair. There were ten minutes remaining before the intelligence meeting. He rubbed the tips of his fingers heavily across his eyelids and stood up—he hated intelligence meetings because he resented, distrusted and—secretly—feared and despised the vast power of the KGB. He recalled the "mysterious" crash of a plane carrying top-level Soviet naval officers not long before the war had begun—*if* it had been nothing more than a crash.

Varakov stood up, looked down to his open uniform blouse and stocking feet and shrugged his shoulders. As commanding general, he had some advantages, he reflected. He left the tunic unbuttoned and walked away from his desk. There were long, low, winding stairs at the rear of the hall leading up to the mezzanine that overlooked the central hall, and he took these, slowly under his ponderous overweight, clinging to the rail as he scaled to the top. There were low benches several feet from the mezzanine rail, and he sat on the nearest of these and stared down into the hall. A massive, life-size sculpture dominated the center, of two mastodons fighting to the death. A smile lifted the corner of Varakov's sagging cheeks. One of the mastodons appeared to be winning the struggle for supremacy. But to what avail—mastodon as a species was now extinct, vanished forever from the earth.

Chapter Three

"I've been meaning to ask you," Rubenstein began, wiping his red bandana handkerchief across his high, sweat-dripping forehead. "Out of all those bikes back there at the crash site, why did you take that particular one?"

Rourke leaned forward on the handlebars of his motorcycle, squinting down at the road below them, the intense desert sun rising in waves, visible despite the dark-lensed aviator-framed glasses he wore. "Couple of reasons," Rourke answered, his voice low. "I like Harley Davidsons, I already have a Low Rider like this," and, almost affectionately, Rourke patted the fuel tank between his legs, "back at the survival retreat. It's about the best combination going for off-road and road use—good enough on gas, fast, handles well, lets you ride comfortably. I like it, I guess," he concluded.

"You've got reasons for everything, haven't you, John?"

"Yeah," Rourke said, his tone thoughtful, "I

usually do. And I've got a very good reason why we should check out that truck trailer down there—see?" and Rourke pointed down the sloping hillside and along the road.

"Where?" Rubenstein said, leaning forward on his bike.

"That dark shape on the side of the road; I'll show you when we get there," Rourke said quietly, revving the Harley under him and starting off down the slope, Rubenstein settling himself on the motorcycle he rode and starting after, as Rourke glanced back over his shoulder at the smaller man.

Perspiration dripped from Rourke's face as well as he hauled the Harley up short and waited at the base of the slope for Rubenstein. Lower down, the air was even hotter. He glanced at the fuel gauge on the bike—just a little over half. As he automatically began calculating approximate mileage, Rubenstein skidded to a halt beside him. "You've gotta watch those hills, pal," Rourke said, the corners of his mouth raising in one of his rare smiles.

"Yeah—tell me about it. But I'm gettin' to control it better."

"All right—you are," Rourke said, then cranked his bike into gear and started across the narrow expanse of ground still separating them from the road. Rourke halted a moment as they reached the highway, stared down the road toward the west and started his motorcycle in the direction of his gaze. The sun was just below its zenith, and as far as Rourke was able to tell they were already into Texas and perhaps seventy-five miles or less from El Paso. The wind in his face and hair and across his body from the slipstream of the bike as it cruised along the highway was hot, but it still had some cooling effect on his skin—already he could feel his shirt, sticking to his back with sweat, starting to dry. He glanced into his rearview mirror and could see Paul Rubenstein trying to catch up.

Rourke smiled.

As he zeroed toward the ever-growing dark spot ahead of them on the highway, his mind flashed back to the beginning of the curious partnership between himself and the younger man. Though trained as a physician, Rourke had never practiced. After several years with the CIA in Latin American Covert Operations, his interests in weapons and survival skills had qualified him as an "expert"—he wrote and taught on the subject around the world. Rubenstein had been a junior editor with a trade magazine publisher in New York City—he was an "expert" on pipe fittings and punctuation marks. But they had two important things in common. They had both survived the crash of the rerouted 747—which Rourke had been taking to Atlanta in order to rejoin his wife and children in northeastern Georgia. That night of the thermonuclear war with Russia had seemingly gone on forever. And now Rourke and Rubenstein shared another bond here in the west Texas desert. Both men had to reach the Atlantic southeast. For Paul Rubenstein, there was the chance that his aged parents might still be alive, that St. Petersburg, Florida, had not been a Soviet target and that the violence after the war had not claimed them. For Rourke—in his mind he could see the three faces before him—there was the hope that his wife and two children were alive. The farm where they had lived in northeast Georgia would have survived the bombs that had fallen on Atlanta. But there were the chances of radiation, food shortages, murderous brigands—all of these to contend with. Rourke swallowed hard as he wished again that his wife, Sarah, would have allowed him to teach her some of the skills that now might enable her to stay alive.

Rourke skidded the Harley into a tight left, realizing he was almost past the abandoned truck trailer. He took the bike in a tight circle around it as Rubenstein approached. As he completed the 360 degrees he stopped alongside the younger man's machine. "Common carrier," Rourke said softly. "Abandoned. After we run the Geiger counter over it we can check what's inside—might be something useful. Shut off your bike. I don't think we're gonna find any gas here."

Rourke gave the Geiger counter strapped to the back of his Harley to Rubenstein and watched as the smaller man carefully checked the truck trailer. The radiation level proved normal. Rourke walked up to the double doors at the rear of the trailer and visually inspected the lock.

"You gonna shoot it off?" Rubenstein was asking, suddenly beside him.

Rourke turned and looked at him. "You've gotten awful violent lately, haven't you? We got a prybar?"

"Nothin' big," the other man said.

"Well," Rourke said, drawing the Metalifed Colt Python from the holster on his right hip, "then I guess I'm going to shoot it off. Stand over there," and Rourke gestured back toward the motorcycles. Once

Rubenstein was clear, Rourke took a few steps back, and on angle to the lock, raised the Magn-Na-Ported six-inch barrel on line with the lock and thumbed back the hammer. He touched the first finger of his right hand to the trigger, his fist locked on the Colt Medallion Pachmayr grips, and the .357 Magnum 158-grain semijacketed soft point round slammed into the lock, visibly shattering the mechanism. Rourke holstered the revolver. As Rubenstein started for the lock, Rourke cautioned, "It might be hot," but Rubenstein was already reaching for it, pulling his hand away as his fingers contacted the metal.

"I said it might be hot," Rourke whispered. "Friction." Rourke walked to the edge of the shoulder, bent down and picked up a medium-sized rock, then walked back to the trailer door and knocked the shattered lock off the hasp with the rock. "Now open it," Rourke said slowly.

Rubenstein fumbled the hasp for a moment, then cleared it and tugged on the doors. "You've got to work that bar lock," Rourke advised.

Rubenstein started trying to pivot the bar and Rourke stepped beside him. "Here—watch," and Rourke swung the bar clear, then opened the right-hand door, reached inside and worked the closure on the left-hand door, then opened it as well.

"Just boxes," Rubenstein said, staring inside the truck.

"It's what's in them that counts. We could stand to resupply."

"But isn't that stealing, John?"

"A few days ago, before the war, it was stealing. Now it's foraging. There's a difference," Rourke said quietly, boosting himself onto the rear of the truck trailer.

"What do you want to forage?" Rubenstein said, throwing himself onto the truck then dragging his legs after him.

Rourke, using the Sting IA from its inside-the-pants sheath, cut open the tape on a small box and said, "Well—what do I want to forage? This might be nice." Reaching into the box, he extracted a long rectangular box about as thick as a pack of cigarettes. "Forty-five ACP ammo—it's even my brand and bullet weight—185-grain JHPs."

"Ammunition?"

"Yeah—jobbers or wholesalers use certain common carriers to ship firearms and ammunition to dealers. I'd hoped we'd find some of this. Find yourself some 9 mm Parabellum—may as well stick to solids so you can use it in that MP-40 as well as the Browning High Power you're carrying. If you come across any guns, let me know."

Rourke started working his way through the truck, opening each box in turn unless the label clearly indicated something useless to him. There were no guns, but he found another consignment of ammunition—.357 Magnum, 125-grain semijacketed hollow points. He put several boxes aside in case he didn't find the bullet weight he wanted.

"Hey, John? Why don't we take all of this stuff—all the ammo, I mean?"

Rourke glanced back to Rubenstein. "How are we going to carry it? I can use .308, .223, .45 ACP and .357—and that's too much. I've got ample supplies of ammunition back at the retreat once we get there."

"That's still close to fifteen hundred miles, isn't it?" Rubenstein's voice had suddenly lost all its enthusiasm. Rourke looked at him, saying nothing.

"Hey, John—you want some spare clips—I mean mgazines—for your rifle?"

Rourke looked up. Rubenstein held thirty-round AR-15 magazines in his hands—a half-dozen. "Are they actual Colt?"

Rubenstein stared at the magazines a moment, Rourke saying, "Look on the bottom—on the floor-plate."

"Yeah—they are."

"Take 'em along then," Rourke said.

"You sure this isn't dishonest—I mean that we're not stealing?"

Rourke, opening a box of baby food in small glass jars, said, "This is a war, Paul. A few nights ago, the United States and the Soviet Union had a major nuclear exchange. The United States apparently didn't fare so well. Every place we flew over before the 747 crashed looked hit—the whole Mississippi River area seems to have been saturated. According to that Arizona kid I got on the radio before we crashed, the San Andreas fault line slipped and everything north of San Diego washed into the sea and the tidal waves flooded as far in as Arizona, and there were quakes there. Albuquerque was abandoned after the fire-storm—except for the injured and dying and the wild dogs—you remember them. We shot it out with that gang of renegade bikers who butchered the people we'd left back at the plane while we went to try and get help. Now how would you evaluate all that?"

"No civil authority, no government—every man

for himself. No law at all."

"You're wrong there," Rourke said quietly. "There is law. There's always moral law—but we're not violating that by taking things here that we need in order to survive out there. And the obligation we have is to stay alive—you want to see if your parents made it, I want to find Sarah and the children. So we owe it to ourselves and to them to stay alive. Now go and see if you can find something to use as a sack to carry all this stuff. I'm going to take some of this baby food—it's full of protein and sugar and vitamins."

"I have a little—I mean had—a little nephew back in New York—that," and Rubenstein's voice began noticeably tightening, "that stuff tastes terrible."

"But it can keep us alive," Rourke said, with a note of finality.

Rubenstein started to turn and go out of the trailer, then looked back to Rourke, saying, "John—New York is gone, isn't it? My nephew—his parents. I had a girl. We weren't serious but we might have gotten serious. But it's gone, isn't it?"

Rourke leaned against the wall of the trailer, his hands flat against the wood there, closing his eyes a moment. "I don't know. You want an educated guess, I'd say, yeah, New York is gone. I'm sorry, Paul. But it was probably quick—they couldn't have even tried to evacuate."

"I know—I've been thinking about that. I used to buy a paper from a little guy down on the corner—he was a Russian immigrant. Came here to escape the mess after the Russian revolution—he was just a little boy then. He was always so concerned with his manliness. I remember in the wintertime he never pulled his hat down over his ears and they were red and peeling. His cheeks were that way. I used to say to him, 'Max—why don't you protect your face and ears—you're gonna get frostbite.' But he'd just smile and not say anything. But he spoke English. I guess he's dead too, huh?"

Rourke sighed hard, then bent forward to look into an open box in front of him. He already knew what was inside the box, but he looked there anyway. "I guess he is, Paul."

"Yeah," Rubenstein said, his voice odd-sounding to Rourke. "I guess—" Rourke looked up and Rubenstein was already climbing out of the trailer. Rourke searched the remaining boxes quickly. He found some flashlight batteries, bar-type shaving soap prepacked in small mugs and safety razors and blades. He rubbed the stubble on his face, took a safety razor, as many packs of blades as he could cram in the breast pocket of his sweat-stained blue shirt and one of the mugs and several bars of soap. He found another consignment of ammunition—158 grain semijacketed soft point .357s and took eight boxes of fifty. With it were some .223 solids, and he took several hundred rounds of these as well. He carried what he wanted in two boxes back to the rear of the trailer and helped Rubenstein climb inside with the sack to carry it all. They crammed the sack full and Rourke jumped down to the road, boosting the sack onto his left shoulder and carrying it toward the bikes. Rourke, as Rubenstein climbed down from the truck, said, "We're going to have to split up this load." As Rourke turned toward his bike, he heard Rubenstein's voice and over it the clicking of bolts—

from assault rifles. Without moving he looked up, heard Rubenstein repeat, "John!"

Slowly, Rourke raised to his full height, squinting against the glare through his sunglasses. A dozen men—in some sort of uniform—were on the far side of the road. Slowly, Rourke turned around, and behind him, on Rubenstein's side of the road beside the abandoned truck trailer, were at least a half-dozen more. All the men carried assault rifles of mixed heritages—and all the guns were trained on Rourke and Rubenstein.

"Caught you boys with your fingers in the pie, didn't we?" a voice from Rubenstein's side of the road shouted.

"That's a damned stupid remark," Rourke said, his voice very low.

"You men are under arrest," the voice said, and this time Rourke matched it with a face in the center of the men by the trailer. Fatter than the others, the man's uniform was more complete and military appearing. There was a patch on the man's left shoulder, and as Rourke tried to decipher what it stood for he noticed the duplicate of the patch on most of the uniforms of the other men.

"Who's arresting us?" Rourke asked softly.

"I am Captain Nelson Pincham of the Texas Independent Paramilitary Response Group," the fat man said.

"Ohh," Rourke started, pausing. "I see. The Texas Independent Paramilitary Response Group—the T-I-P-R-G—Tiprg. That sounds stupid."

The self-proclaimed captain took a step forward, saying, "We'll see how stupid it sounds when you boys get shot in just about a minute and a half. Official policy is to shoot looters on sight."

"Is that a fact?" Rourke commented. "Whose official policy is it—yours?"

"It's the official policy of the Paramilitary Provisional Government of Texas."

"Try saying that sometime with a couple of beers under your belt," Rourke said, staring at Pincham.

"Drop that sidearm," Pincham said. "That big hogleg on the belt around your waist. Move, boy!" Pincham commanded.

Out of the corner of his eye Rourke could already see hands reaching out and taking Rubenstein's High Power from the holster slung to his pants belt. The Schmeisser, as Rubenstein still called it, and Rourke's CAR-15 and Steyr-Mannlicher SSG were still on the bikes. Rourke slowly reached to the buckle of the Ranger Leather belt at his waist and loosened it, holding the tongue of the belt in his right hand away from his body. One of the troopers stepped forward and grabbed it, then stepped back.

"Now the guns from the shoulder holsters—quick," Pincham said, his voice sounding more confident.

Slowly, Rourke started to reach up to the harness, then Pincham shouted, "Hold it!" The captain turned to the trooper nearest him and barked, "Go get those pistols—move out!"

The trooper walked toward Rourke. "You sure you don't want to talk about this—you're just going to shoot us?" Rourke asked softly.

"I'm sure," Pincham said, his face breaking into a grin.

Rourke just nodded his head, keeping his hands away from the twin stainless Detonics .45s in their double shoulder rig. The trooper was in front of him now, between Rourke and Pincham and the rest of the men on the trailer side of the road. The trooper rasped, "Now—take out both those shiny pistols, mister. Just reach under your armpits there nice and slow—the right hand gets the one under the right arm, the left hand the left one. Nice and easy, then stick 'em out in front of you with the pistol butts toward me."

"Right," Rourke said quietly. As he reached up for the guns, he said, "To get them out of the holsters, I've got to jerk them a little bit."

"You just watch how you do it, mister. No funny stuff or I cut you in half where you stand." Rourke eyed the H-K assault rifle in the man's hands.

Rourke reached for his guns, his hands moving slowly. He curled the last three fingers of each hand on the Pachmayr gripped butts of the Detonics pistols and jerked them free of the leather. Rourke eyed the trooper, who was visibly tense as the guns cleared, and slowly brought them forward in his hands, the butts of the guns facing toward the "soldier."

"That's a good boy," the trooper said, smiling. The trooper took his left hand from the front stock of his rifle and reached forward for the gun in Rourke's right hand.

The corners of Rourke's mouth raised in a smile. Rourke's hands dropped to waist level, the twin stainless .45s spinning on his index fingers in the trigger guards, the pistol butts arcing into his fists, his thumbs snapping back the hammers and both pistols firing simultaneously, one slug pumping into the trooper's throat, the second grazing his shoulder as it hammered past and into the chest of the soldier closest to Paul Rubenstein. Rourke pumped two shots into the men on the far side of the road and dove toward the trailer, rolling under it, firing both pistols into the men flanking Captain Pincham. Out of the corner of his eye, Rourke could see Rubenstein—almost as if in slow motion. The smaller man had done just what Rourke had hoped—he'd grabbed up an assault rifle from the man nearest him whom Rourke had shot down and now had the muzzle of the weapon flush against Pincham's right cheekbone. Rourke stopped firing as he heard Rubenstein shouting, "Hold your fire or Pincham gets his!"

Rourke crawled the rest of the way along under the truck and got his feet on the other side, two rounds each still in the twin .45s. He leveled them both across the road, ignoring the men near him. "Your show, Paul," Rourke almost whispered, catching Rubenstein's eye.

He watched the younger man nod, then heard him shout, "Now everybody get out from cover and throw your rifles to the ground—move it or Pincham gets this. Move it!"

Rourke watched as Rubenstein shoved the muzzle of the assault rifle against Pincham's cheek, heard Pincham shout, "Do as they say—hurry!"

Slowly, the men on the far side of the road climbed out of the ditch they'd dropped into as Rourke had opened up on them. Rourke watched as, one by one, they dropped their rifles, hearing the rifles from the man near Rubenstein and Pincham clattering to the ground beside him. "Gunbelts too," Rubenstein shouted.

Rourke watched as the men started dropping their pistol belts to the ground. His eyes scanned the ground and he saw his own gunbelt there, then he stepped toward it and bent down, breaking the thumb snap on the flap over the Python. He shook the holster free and let it fall to the ground, the Detonics from his right hand already in his trouser belt, the long-tubed, vent-ribbed Python now in his right. Thumbing the hammer back, he walked slowly across the road, his long strides putting him beside the man in the center of the ten men still standing there. Glancing down to the ground, he spotted the two he'd killed. Sticking the muzzle of the Python against the temple of the closest man, Rourke almost whispered, "All right—you guys want to be military—get into the front leaning rest position. That's like a pushup, but you don't go down. Now!"

Rourke stepped back, guiding the man closest to him down to the ground. The ten got to their knees, arms outstretched, then balanced on their toes as they stretched their legs, supporting themselves on their hands. "First man moves dies," Rourke said quietly, starting back across the road.

He could hear Rubenstein shouting similar commands to the men with Pincham on the trailer side of the road. Rourke looked at Rubenstein, hearing the younger man say, "What do we do now?"

"You want to kill them?"

"What?"

"Neither do I, especially. Why don't you get the bikes straight in a minute here and we can take these fellas for a walk a few miles down the road, then let 'em go. Let me reload first—keep them covered." Rourke jammed the Python in his belt, changed magazines on both of the .45s and reholstered them. He caught up his pistol belt from the dirt and slung it over his shoulder, the Python back in his right fist. Already, Rubenstein had begun dividing the loads for the bikes.

"You guys got any vehicles around here?" Rourke asked Pincham. The captain said nothing. Rourke put the muzzle of the Python under his nose.

"Yes—on both sides of the road."

"Any gas cans?"

"Yes—yes," Pincham snapped.

"Much obliged," Rourke said, then, shouting, "Paul—go over there and get some gas for the bikes. Take that thing you call a Schmeisser in case they left someone on guard. Did you leave anyone on guard?" Rourke asked, lowering his voice and eyeing Pincham.

"No—no-nobody on guard!"

"Good—if anything happens to my friend, you get an extra nostril."

"Nobody on guard!" Pincham said again, his voice sounding higher each time he spoke.

After a few moments, Rubenstein returned with the gas cans, filled the bikes and mounted up. Rourke walked Pincham toward his own bike. Already, some of the troopers were starting to fall, unable to support themselves on their hands.

"Barbarian," Pincham growled.

"No," Rourke said quietly. "I just want them good and tired so they can't get back here fast enough to follow us. It's either that or we disable your vehicles. And I don't think you'd like being stranded out here in the desert on foot. Right?"

Pincham, biting his lower lip, only nodded.

"All right—captain," Rourke said. "Order your men onto their feet and get 'em walking ahead of us—you bring up the rear. Anyone tries anything, it's your problem." Rourke started his bike as Pincham got his men up, formed them in a ragged column of twos and started them down the road toward El Paso.

As Rourke and Rubenstein followed along behind them, Rourke glancing at the Harley's odometer coming up on the second mile, Pincham—walking laboriously, close in front of him—said, "Mister—you killed three of my men."

"Four," Rourke corrected.

"If I ever catch sight of you, you're a dead man."

"There's some great baby food back there in the truck in case you fellas get hungry," Rourke responded, then to Rubenstein, "Let's go Paul!" Rourke gunned the Harley between his legs and shot past Pincham and his column, Rubenstein on the other side close behind him. Past the paramilitary troops now, Rourke glanced over his shoulder—some of Pincham's men were already sitting along the side of the road. Pincham was standing there, shaking his fist down the road after Rourke.

Rubenstein, beside Rourke, was shouting over the rush of air. "I saw that trick in a western movie once—with the pistols, I mean."

Rourke just nodded.

"What do they call it, John, where you roll the guns like that when someone tries taking them?"

Rourke glanced across at Rubenstein, then bent over his bike a little to get a more comfortable position. "The road-agent spin," Rourke said.

"Road-agent spin," Rubenstein echoed. "Wow!"

Chapter Four

Varakov was pleased that he had ordered the intelligence briefing to be in his office at the side of the long central hall. The desk was closed in the front, and with the chairs arranged in a semicircle no one could see his feet. He wiggled his toes in his white boot socks and leaned back in his chair. "There are several other priorities aside from the elimination of political undesirables," he said flatly.

"Moscow wants—" the KGB man, Major Vladmir Karamatsov, began.

"Moscow wants me to run this country, keep armed rebellion from getting out of hand—some resistance cannot be avoided in a nation where everyone owns a gun—and try to get the heavy industry restarted. That is what Moscow wants. How I choose to accomplish that is my concern. If Moscow eventually decides I am not doing my job properly, then I will be replaced. This will not," and Varakov crashed his hamlike fist down on the desk—"be a fiefdom of the KGB. Intelligence is to serve the interests of the Soviet people and the government—the government and the people are not holding their breath to serve the interest of intelligence. The Soviet is facing famine, a shortage of raw materials and most of our heavy industry has been destroyed by American missiles. If we cannot get this new land we have acquired to be productive, we shall all starve, have no more ammunition for our guns, have no spare parts. Most of American heavy industry is intact. Most of ours is gone. Our primary responsibility is to man the factories with work battalions and develop productivity. Otherwise, all is lost."

Varakov looked around the room, his eyes stopping a moment on Captain Natalia Tiemerovna, also KGB and Karamatsov's most trusted and respected agent. "What do you think, captain?" Varakov asked, his voice softening.

He watched the woman as she moved uneasily in her chair, her uniform skirt sliding up over her knees a moment, a wave of her dark hair falling across her forehead as she looked up to speak. Varakov watched as she brushed the hair away from her deep blue eyes. "Comrade general, I realize the importance of the tasks you have enumerated. But in order to successfully reactivate industry here, we must be secure against sabotage and organized subversion. Comrade Major Karamatsov, I am sure, only wishes to begin working to eliminate potential subversives from the master list in order to speed on your goals, comrade general."

"You should have been a diplomat—Natalia. It is Natalia, is it not?"

"Yes, comrade general," the girl answered, her

voice a rich alto. Varakov liked her voice best of all.

"There is one small matter," Varakov began, "before we get to your master list of persons for liquidation. It is not an intelligence matter, but I wish your collective input. The bodies. In the neutron-bombed areas such as Chicago, there are rotting corpses everywhere. Wild dogs and cats have come in from the areas that were not bombed. Rats are becoming a problem—a serious problem. Public health, comrades. Any suggestions? I cannot have you arrest and liquidate rats, bacteria and wolflike hounds."

"There are many natives in the unaffected parts of the city that were suburban to the city itself," Karamatsov said. "And—"

Varakov cut him off. "I knew somehow, comrade major, that you would have a plan."

Karamatsov nodded slightly and continued. "We can send troops into these areas to form these people into work battalions, designating central areas for burning of corpses and equipping some of these work battalions with chemical agents to destroy the rats and bacteria."

"But, Vladmir," Captain Tiemerovna began. Then starting again, "But comrade major, such chemicals, to be effective, must be in sufficient strength that those persons in the work battalions could be adversely affected by them."

"Precautions will of course be taken, but there will be adequate replacements for those who become careless, Natalia," Karamatsov said, dismissing the remark. Turning to Varakov, then standing and walking toward the edge of the semicircle, then turning abruptly around—Varakov supposed for dramatic effect—Karamatsov said, "But once these work battalions have completed their task, they can be organized into factory labor. If they are utilized in twelve-hour shifts, working through the night—the electrification system is still largely intact—the city can be reclaimed within days. A week at the most. I can have the exact figures for you within the hour, comrade general," and he snapped his heels together. Varakov did not like that—Karamatsov reminded him too much of Nazis from the Second War.

"I do not think your figures will be necessary—but unfortunately your plan seems to be the most viable," Varakov said.

"Thank you, comrade general, but providing the figures will be of no difficulty. I had anticipated that this problem might be of concern to you and have already had them prepared, pending of course the actual number of survivors available for the work battalions and the quantities of chemical equipment that can be secured for the program—but I can easily obtain these additional figures, should you so desire."

Varakov nodded his head, hunching low over his desk, staring at Karamatsov. "I am not ready to retire yet, my ambitious young friend."

"I assure you, comrade general," Karamatsov began, walking toward Varakov's desk.

"Nothing is assured, Karamatsov—but now tell me about your list."

Karamatsov sat down, then stood again and walked to the opposite end of the semicircle of chairs occupied by KGB and military officials. Turning abruptly—once again for dramatic flair, Varakov supposed—Karamatsov blurted out, "We must protect the safety of the State at all costs, comrades. And of course it is for this reason that many years ago—before the close of World War Two—my predecessors began the compilation of a list—constantly updated—of persons who in the event of war with the capitalist superpowers would be potential troublemakers, rallying points for resistance, etc. The master list, as it came to be called, has, as I indicated, been constantly updated. It was impossible to predict with any acceptable degree of accuracy who might survive such a war and who might not, and to determine which targets would be most readily able to be eliminated in any event. For this reason, since its inception, the master list was broken into broad categories of persons—all of equal value for elimination purposes."

"These are names we might recognize?" Varakov interrupted.

"Oh, yes—comrade general, many of these names are important public officials. Yet many of the other names are not so easily recognized—except to us!"

"Give to me some examples of this, major," Varakov interrupted again.

"Well—they are from all areas of life. In the Alpha section for example, one of the most important names is Samuel Chambers," Karamatsov said. "This Chambers person, as best as we can ascertain, is the only surviving member of something called the presidential Cabinet. He was the minister—secretary, that is—of communications. According to our interpretation of the American Constitution, he is, in fact, whether he knows it or not, the president of the United States at this moment. He must be eliminated. Chambers is an excellent example. He was in the Beta section until his elevation to the Alpha section corresponding with his elevation to the presidential advisory Cabinet. He has always been ardently opposed to our country—an anticommunist he called himself. He has always had a great popular support because of this position. He owned several radio and television broadcasting stations, had a radio program broadcast on independently owned radio stations around the country for several years—his name was a household word, as the Americanism goes."

"This homeheld word—he is president now? Then do we not wish to negotiate formal surrender with him?" Varakov asked, forcing his voice to sound patient, interested.

"Under normal circumstances, yes, comrade general—we would. But, this Chambers would never agree. And, if we forced his signing of a conciliatory statement, the people here would never accept its validity. His only value is as a dead man. In his very utility as a symbol of American anticommunist feeling, his death would be but another blow to American resistance, showing them how useless such activity is—how counterproductive."

"Give me still another example," Varakov said, killing time for himself until the situation demanded he give Karamatsov formal orders to begin working on the list—he did not like ordering people to die. He had trained as a soldier too long to value life as cheaply as did the KGB.

"I—yes," Karamatsov said, pacing across the room between the semicircle of chairs and Varakov's desk. "Yes—a good example. I have no inclination that the man is still alive. He was a writer, living in the American southeast. Adventure novels about American terrorists fighting communist agents from the Soviet Union and other countries. He wrote often as well in magazines devoted to sporting firearms. Several times he openly condemned our system of government in print in national periodicals here. He attempted to exalt individualism and subvert the purposes of social order through his articles and his books—his name I do not recall at this point in time. He would be on a low-priority list, but nonetheless his liquidation would be necessary.

"Still another example would be retired Central Intelligence Agency personnel who remained provisionally active. Reserve officers in the armed forces would be still another list. There are many thousands of names, Comrade General Varakov, and work must be begun immediately to locate and liquidate these persons as potential subversives."

Varakov slowly, emphatically and quite softly, said, "Purge?"

"Yes—but a purge for the ultimate furthering of the collective purposes of the heroic Soviet people, comrade general!"

Varakov looked at Karamatsov, then glanced to Natalia Tiemerovna. She was moving uncomfortably in the folding chair. He looked back to Karamatsov, watched as Karamatsov watched him. "I will sign this order," Varakov almost whispered. "But since individual execution orders would not be necessary, I will have it amended to read that only such persons as currently are named on the master list can be liquidated without express written order, signed by myself." Coughing, Varakov added, "I do not wish to initiate a bloodbath." Then looking at Karamatsov, staring at the younger man's coal-black eyes and the intensity there, Varakov extended the first finger of his right hand, pointing it at Karamatsov, and said, "Make no mistake that I will be so foolish as to sign a blanket order that could someday be turned into my own death warrant, comrade."

Chapter Five

The red-orange orb of sun was low on the horizon at the far end of the long straight ribbon of flat highway reaching toward El Paso, still some ten or more miles away, as Rourke figured it. He turned his bike onto the shoulder and braked, arcing the front wheel to the side and resting on it, looking down the road. He didn't bother to turn as Rubenstein pulled up beside him, overshooting Rourke by a few feet, then walking the bike back. "Why are we stopping, John?"

"We're about eight or ten minutes out of El Paso. It doesn't look like it was hit. But it wasn't what you might call the gentlest town in the world before the war, I remember. Juarez is right across the bridge from it over the Rio Grande."

"We going into Mexico?"

"No—not unless I can't avoid it. Those paramilitary troops we locked horns with were bad enough to worry about and they're on our tail by now again. Probably had a radio, right?"

"Yeah," Rubenstein said, looking thoughtful a moment. "Yeah, I think they did."

"Well, we might have a reception waiting for us up ahead. But in Mexico we could have federal troops on our tails—they do their number a hell of a lot better. With the guns and the bikes and whatever other equipment somebody might imagine we had, we'd have everybody and his brother trying to knock us off to get it. I don't know if Mexico got caught up in the war or not, but things might be awful rough down there."

"Well," Rubenstein said, "maybe we should skip El Paso entirely."

"Yeah, I've thought of that," Rourke said slowly, still staring down the highway. He lit one of his cigars and tongued it to the left corner of his mouth. "I thought about that a lot on the road the last few miles. But I haven't seen any game since we got started, have you?"

Rubenstein looked at him, then quickly said, "No—me neither."

Rourke just nodded, then said, "And that baby food I snatched isn't going to make more than a day's rations for both of us. And you're right, it does taste kind of pukey. We need food, we're almost out of water and we could use some more gasoline. I wouldn't mind scrounging some medical instruments if I could find them. I've got all that stuff at the retreat, but it's a long way getting there still."

"You never told me," Rubenstein asked, staring down the highway trying to see what Rourke was staring at so intently. "Why do you have the retreat? I mean, did you know this war was going to happen, or what?"

"No—I didn't know it," Rourke said slowly. "See, I went through medical school, interned and everything. I'd always been interested in history, current events, things like that." Rourke exhaled a long stream of gray cigar smoke that caught on the light breeze and eddied in front of him a moment before vanishing into the air. "I guess I figured that instead of training to cure people's problems, maybe I could prevent them. Didn't work out though. I joined the CIA, spent some years there—mostly in Latin America. I was always good with guns, liked the out-of-doors. Some experiences I had with the company sort of sharpened my skills that way. I married Sarah just before I got out. I was already writing about survival and weapons training—things like that. I settled down to writing and started the retreat. The more friction that developed between us, the more time and energy I poured into the retreat. I've got a couple of years' worth of food and other supplies there, the facilities to grow more food, make my own ammo. The water supply is abundant—I even get my electricity from it. All the comforts—" Rourke stopped in midsentence.

"All the comforts of home," Rubenstein volunteered brightly, completing the sentence.

"Once I find Sarah and Michael and Ann."

"How old is Michael again?"

"Michael's six," Rourke said, "and little Annie just turned four. Sarah's thirty-two. That picture I showed you of Sarah and the kids is kind of off—but it was a kind of happy time when I took it so I held on to it."

"She's an artist?"

"Illustrated children books, then started writing them too a couple of years ago. She's very good at it."

"I always wanted to try my hand at being an artist," Rubenstein said.

Rourke turned and glanced at Rubenstein, saying nothing.

"What do you think we'll run into in El Paso?" Rubenstein asked, changing the subject.

"Something unpleasant, I'm sure," Rourke said, exhaling hard and chomping down on his cigar. He unlimbered the CAR-15 with the collapsible stock and three-power scope and slung it under his right arm, then cradled the gun across hs lap. He worked the bolt to chamber a round and set the safety, then started the Harley.

"Better get yours," he said to Rubenstein, nodding toward the German MP-40 submachinegun strapped to the back of Rubenstein's bike.

"I guess I'd better," the smaller man said, pushing his glasses up off the bridge of his nose. "Hey, John?"

"Paul?"

"I did okay back there, didn't I—I mean with those paramilitary guys?"

"You did just fine."

"I mean, I'm not just hangin' on with you, am I?"

Rourke smiled, saying, "If you were, Paul, I'd tell you." Rourke cranked into gear and started slowly along the shoulder. Rubenstein—Rourke glanced back—already had the "Schmeisser" slung under his right arm and was jumping his bike.

Chapter Six

Sarah Rourke reined back on Tildie, her chestnut mare, pulling up short behind Carla Jenkins' bay. Sarah watched Carla closely, and the little girl Millie astride behind her. To Sarah Rourke's thinking, Carla handled a horse like she handled a shopping cart—she was dangerous with either one. Leaning over in the saddle, Sarah glanced past Carla to Carla's husband, Ron, the retired army sergeant to whom she had temporarily entrusted her fate and the fate of the children. The children . . . she looked back over her shoulder at Michael and Annie sitting astride her husband John's horse. The big off-white mare with the black stockings and black mane and tail was named "Sam," and she reached back and stroked Sam's muzzle now, saying to the children, "How are you guys doing? Isn't it fun riding Daddy's horse?"

"His saddle's too big, Momma," Michael said.

Annie added, "I want to ride with you, Mommie. I don't like riding on Sam—she's not soft." Annie looked like she was going to cry—for the hundredth time, Sarah reminded herself.

"Later—you can ride with me later, Annie. Now just be good. I want to find out why Mr. Jenkins stopped." Sarah turned in her saddle, standing up in the stirrups to peer past Carla again. She couldn't see Jenkins' face, just the back of his head, the thick set of his shoulders and neck, and the dark rump of the appaloosa gelding he rode.

"What's the problem, Ron?" Sarah asked, trying not to shout in case there were some danger ahead.

"No problem, Sarah, at least not yet," Jenkins said, not turning to face her. Hearing Ron Jenkins call her by her first name still sounded odd to her, but she reminded herself she had never called him Ron until a few days ago when he and his wife and daughter had come to the farm and asked if she wanted to accompany them. They moved slowly, the Jenkins family, and Ron Jenkins had meticulously avoided every possible small town between them and "the mountains" he kept referring to. But they were already in the mountains, she realized, and she wondered if Jenkins' enigmatic references had been to the Smoky Mountains of Tennessee rather than the mountains of northwestern Georgia. Leaning back in the saddle, trying to press her spine against the cantle to relieve the aching, she realized that if Jenkins intended to take them out of Georgia she would not go. On the chance that her husband, John, was still alive—and somewhere she told herself, as she had told the children repeatedly, that he was—chances would be slimmer of his finding them if they left the state and the area around the farm. She knew that her husband's survival retreat was in these mountains somewhere, and if they stayed in them it would only be a matter of time, if—*when,* she reminded herself—he came for them, before they would meet. But the farther Jenkins took her away from the northeast Georgia farm she and the children had called home before the night of the war, the slimmer the chances would be.

They had viewed some towns from a distance, and many had looked as though they had been looted and burned. Once, several hours back, they had hidden quietly as a gang of brigands, on motorcycles and driving pickup trucks, had gone down along a road they had been about to cross.

Sarah's mind flashed back to the night of the war, and to the morning after and the gunfight when she had killed the men and the woman who had tried to harm her and the children. Her spine shivered and she twisted involuntarily in the saddle, her eyes drifting to the much modified AR-15 rifle she had taken from one of the dead men. Her husband's Colt .45 was still in the trouser band of her Levis and she shifted it—the automatic was rubbing against her flesh and it hurt.

Checking the reins for Sam knotted to her saddle horn, she loosed them again and pulled her husband's horse after her as she passed Carla Jenkins' bay and rode up alongside Ron. "What is it, Ron?" she asked again.

"Down there—another town," he answered.

Sarah looked where he pointed, catching a loose strand of hair and tucking it under the blue and white bandanna covering her head. Her hair felt dirty to her—she had not washed it since the morning before the war. There hadn't been enough water and there hadn't been any time.

It was already nearly dusk and she couldn't see clearly at first in the sunlight-obscured shallow valley below them, but after a moment, as her eyes became more accustomed to the dimness, she could make out the scene unfolding there. It was the brigand gang they had seen several hours earlier. The faces were strange when she had seen them from quite close then, but even discounting that, she had known they were not from the area. People in Georgia were, by and large, good-natured, gentle people. As a northerner in a strange part of the country she had learned that years earlier. And these men and women in the small town below them were not gentle. Some of the old frame houses on both ends of the main street were already afire. The bulk of the gang of brigands was in the center of the town. Looking down into the shallow valley, she was too far away to make out individual actions, but—rather like large ants—she could see them moving from store to store in the small business district. Because of the clearness of the mountain air, she could even hear the sounds of smashing glass from the shop windows. She could hear shots as well.

"Those people were fools to stay in their town," Jenkins observed to her.

"Well, can't we do something, Mr. Jenkins?" The formality of the way she addressed him shocked her.

"Well, Mrs. Rourke," and his voice emphasized her name, "I'm no weapons expert like your husband was."

"Is—Mr. Jenkins."

"I doubt that. I think he bought it during the war. Atlanta I figure is just one big crater right now and you said yourself he was supposed to be landin' there. But I ain't like him whether he's alive or dead—I'm just an army veteran tryin' to get along. I can handle a gun as good as the next man, but I'm not about to go racin' on down there and be a hero 'cause all I'll be is dead and you and my wife and daughter and your kids then is gonna be just on your own. And that ain't right. I got a responsibility to my family and to your family. And I take that pretty serious."

Involuntarily almost, she reached across and pressed Jenkins' hand. "I'm sorry," she said softly. "You're right, I guess."

She glanced back over her shoulder and noticed Carla Jenkins staring at her.

She took her hand away from Ron Jenkins' hand.

"What are we going to do, then?" she asked him.

"I think we're gonna just sit tight up here and see which way them folks decides to go after they finish their business down there. Then we'll move out in the opposite direction. Carla's got a sister up in the Smokies there around Mount Eagle and I reckon that should be a pretty safe place to go."

"But that's in Tennessee, Mr. Jenkins—I can't go there!"

"Mrs. Rourke. Now listen," and Jenkins for the first time faced her, turning in the saddle and getting eye contact with her. "I don't know what's under that scarf and all that hair and everythin' and hidin' there in the back of your pretty little head, ma'am, but you can't just sit out here in the mountains and wait for your husband to appear out of nowhere now and rescue you. You got them two kids to look out for same as I got my wife and daughter. Once things calm down a might after everythin' gets settled, you can always look for your husband then. But if you decide on stayin' in these mountains with the likes of them down here," and he gestured toward the pillaging in the town below them, "you ain't gonna last a day—and that's a pure fact."

"But my husband will never find us in Tennessee."

"Your husband is dead, Mrs. Rourke—and I wish you'd wake up and see that."

Sarah Rourke looked at him suddenly, pulling the bandanna from her head, realizing it was giving her a headache. She said, her voice low and even, "John is alive, Mr. Jenkins. I've been telling that to my children and I believe it myself. He spent his whole life learning how to stay alive and I know he did somehow. And I know that somewhere now wherever he is he's thinking about me and about Michael and Annie and risking everything to get back here to us. And I'm not going to betray him and run out. I'm not. He's alive. John is alive and you can't tell me otherwise, Mr. Jenkins. And I'm not going to Tennessee with you or anyone else."

She twisted the bandanna in her hands, then stared down into the valley. As the sunlight ebbed, she could see the fires at both ends of the town much more clearly.

Chapter Seven

All Ron Jenkins had said to her and to his wife, Carla, was, "I'm goin' on down into that town there. I won't need my horse—you keep it close by and saddled and ready. I figure they might have some water and some other things down there I reckon we could use just as soon as letting them down there to rot."

Carla Jenkins had thrown her arms around her husband and tried to stop him, but one thing Sarah Rourke had learned about Ron Jenkins was that once he made up his mind he wouldn't change it. She remembered her own husband being like that, but now, since the night of the war and her experiences that following morning, she felt that perhaps she should have changed hers. She had hated the guns he kept, practically called him a fool for building and stocking his survival retreat. Yet, guns had kept her alive so far, and now the survival retreat she had loathed the thought of seemed to her a sort of haven of normalcy as she sat there in the dark, huddled with the children, their heads on her lap.

There could be no fire, the brigands having left the town only a few hours earlier and still perhaps close enough to see a fire and come and investigate. She couldn't sleep, though she was tired. Her body was beyond sleep, she thought. She watched Carla Jenkins. Carla—who talked too much usually—was silent as a grave, her daughter Millie's head cradled on her lap. Carla—less than a yard away from Sarah—just sat staring out into the darkness.

The sound came again, and the shiver up Sarah Rourke's spine came again as well. It was a scream, from the town below them in the darkness of the valley. A scream, but an unnatural-sounding one. She knew the sound, having worked as a volunteer in a hospital where she'd first met John Rourke. It was a man screaming. She had heard the sound in the hospital emergency room too often. She had met John, thought little beyond the fact that his lean face and high forehead and dark eyes and hair looked attractive and that he had apparently noticed her too. Years later, when their lives had crossed again, they had dated, talked a lot and married eventually. It had taken both of them some time to recall the chance meeting years earlier. They had laughed about it.

But now, as the scream came for a third time, the memory of each moment shared with her husband was like a cocoon to which she could withdraw, even if just for an instant.

Finally, when the scream came a fourth time, she eased the children's heads from her lap, pushed the hair from Michael's eyes and moved nearer to Carla Jenkins. "I think one of us should go and see, Carla,"

Sarah whispered, afraid that even the slightest noise might attract the brigands.

"I can't," Carla answered, her voice barely audible.

"I can go," Sarah said, bolstering her courage and simultaneously cursing herself for having said it.

"No—you mustn't. Ron will be back soon."

"But someone is screaming down there, Carla. It might be that something has happened—"

"No—he is just fine. Now you let things be."

Sarah Rourke sat back on her haunches, staring at Carla Jenkins, seeing the face, watching the lips move even in the darkness between them—but hearing herself. She couldn't say to Carla Jenkins, "You're being a fool—your husband is in trouble down there. The brigands must have come back—they're killing him." She couldn't say that without admitting to herself that perhaps the thought of John Rourke coming for her and Michael and Annie was just a fantasy.

"I'm going," she said finally.

"I don't want you to."

"Watch Michael and Annie, Carla—I have to—" but Sarah Rourke didn't finish the sentence. The scream came for a fifth time, only weaker but longer in duration now. She stood up, checked the .45 Colt Government Model in her waistband and went back to Michael and Ann. She nudged Michael. "Michael—I need you to wake up."

"No—I wasn't asleep. Just a—"

"Now Michael—you're like your father! The slightest noise in the middle of the night and you're wide awake. Try to wake you up in the morning and it's like World War—" She stopped, her mouth still open. My God, she thought! How we used to joke about it. She tried waking Michael again and this time he sat up.

"Now, are you awake?"

"Yes," he said, his voice not sounding that way to her.

"All right—I'm going down into the valley to see if Mr. Jenkins is all right. I don't want to wake up Annie, but if she does wake up keep her very still. If she makes noise those bad men who burned the town there could find us. Do you understand, Michael?"

"Yes, I understand. But why do you have to go, Mom?"

"Somebody has to go—Mr. Jenkins might be in trouble down there."

"Do you have your gun—so you can shoot them if you have to?"

She looked at her son, running her fingers in his hair. His hair, his face, even the dark eyes that because of the night she couldn't quite see were exactly like her husband's. She was coming to understand that so was his logic. "Yes, I'll take my gun. Just listen to Mrs. Jenkins and do what she says unless—" and Sarah Rourke looked over her shoulder, watched Carla Jenkins staring into the darkness, rock rigid. "Unless what she says doesn't sound right—do you understand what I mean?"

He screwed up his face, looked away a moment, then said, "I think I do—if she tells me to do something dumb, I shouldn't do it?"

"Right—but think—just think and otherwise do

what she says."

He leaned up and put his arms around her neck and she kissed him, barely touching her left hand to her daughter's head in fear of waking her. "Take care of Annie—remember you're the man," she said.

Sarah Rourke reached down and took the AR-15, checked the safety and pulled the bandanna down a little over her ears. She blew Michael a kiss and started away from the campsite. She half thought of taking her horse as a quick means of escape, but the noise the animal would make might give her away, she reasoned. The legs of her jeans—bell bottoms—caught continuously on the brush as she moved as silently as she could into the woods on the slope and down into the valley. She stopped after a few hundred yards and rolled up the cuffs of her pants. She heard another scream; by now she had lost count. She remembered reading a western novel her husband had bought once. In it, the Indians had taken the scout captive and were torturing him throughout the night and into the early morning, just to unnerve the settlers hiding in the circled wagon train. They had tied the man to a wagon wheel and roasted him over a fire. The thought of it still caused her to shudder.

She stopped in her tracks, then dropped to the ground, hugging the AR-15 to her chest. She was less than a hundred yards from the main street of the town now and could see the center of the street clearly. She could see a half-dozen or so of the brigands—and at their center she could see Ron Jenkins. At least she supposed it was Ron Jenkins. She heard the scream again and almost screamed herself.

One of the men—a tall black man with no sleeves on his coat—had a jumper cable in his gloved right hand, the cable leading to a storage battery on the ground a few inches from Ron Jenkins' feet. When he touched the end of the cable to Jenkins' body, Jenkins twisted against the ropes binding him to the front bumper of the pickup truck, shuddered, then screamed again.

Sarah Rourke looked carefully on each side of the center of the street and saw no one—just the four men and two women torturing Ron Jenkins. One of the men was black, as was one of the women. There was another pickup truck parked a few yards away from the one to which Ron Jenkins was lashed, but it appeared empty to her. She moved the selector of the AR-15 to the unmarked full-auto position—the gun had been illegally altered by the man she'd taken it from.

She got up to her knees, then rose to her feet, the rifle snugged to her shoulder.

"Don't move—any of you. I've got you covered with an automatic rifle," she announced at the top of her lungs. "Now step away from him!"

"Well, well," the black man shouted back, turning to face her. "We cut your sign earlier—figured if we grabbed your man here you'd soon come along to get him. You can have him too, all we want is your horses—and maybe somethin' else. He don't look like much for a girl like you—tits like I bet you got under that T-shirt I guess could set a fella like me just on fire, sweet thing." The black man laughed, then started walking toward her. "Now, gimme that ol' gun before I whip your white ass with it for being bad to me, hear?"

Sarah Rourke touched her finger to the trigger of the modified AR-15 and shot the black man in the face, then brought the muzzle around and started firing at the remaining three men and two women. They started to run, only one of them starting to shoot back at her. She fired at him and he threw both his hands up to his face.

She shot one of the women in the back as the woman tried making it into the pickup truck, shot another of the men in the head as he jumped into the back of the furthest truck, which was already in motion. The black woman was in the cab. The last man was running to catch it and Sarah fired, a three-shot burst which she felt—oddly—proud of herself for being able to control. She'd drawn a three-point bullet hole line across the man's back and he'd fallen forward on his face as the truck had sped away.

She almost automatically changed magazines for the rifle, set the selector back to safe and took the pistol out, her thumb over the raised safety catch, the hammer cocked. She ran to Ron Jenkins, glancing over the dead as she did to make sure they were dead.

She dropped to her knees beside him, setting the AR-15 onto the ground and raising his head with her left hand. "Ron—it's all right. I'll get you out of this," she said.

Eyes opened and staring past her, she could hear him whisper, "I'm not gonna—gonna make it, Mrs. Rourke. Take care of Carla and Millie—get 'em to Mount Eagle. God bless you—'cause them killers is gonna be back here sure as I'm—" and his eyes kept staring but there was a rattling sound in his throat and his breath suddenly smelled bad to her. She took her hand from his face, got to her feet and stepped a pace back. She stared at him a moment. "You're dead—Mr. Jenkins," she said hoarsely. "You're dead."

Chapter Eight

There was gunfire by the border crossing, Rourke decided as he turned his motorcycle into the side street and pulled up alongside the curb.

"What's all that shooting?" Rubenstein queried.

"Either some of them—Mexicans—are trying to get across the border into here—which would be damned foolish just now—or a pile of Americans are trying to get across into Mexico—which would be just the reverse of the usual situation, wouldn't it. White Anglo-Saxon Protestant wetbacks."

"Jess—you were right about this place. Everything," and Rubenstein turned around in his seat and stared at the buildings lining both sides of the street, "looks like it's been looted fifty times."

"Somethin' to do, I guess," Rourke commented, staring behind them, as if somehow he could watch the gunfight around the corner and beyond. Then, turning and looking up the street ahead of them, Rourke whispered, "Quiet a minute."

The sound was a rumbling, growing louder by the

second, it seemed. "What is it?" Rubenstein asked, staring into the empty street.

"Shh!" Rourke whispered. He was silent for another moment, then slowly, glancing behind him, said to Rubenstein, "Sounds like a riot maybe—some kind of a mob heading toward us. Let's get out of here." Rourke started turning his bike, Rubenstein behind him. Glancing up the street, Rourke watched as the mob turned into it—men, women, even some children, hands and arms flailing in the air, some carrying clubs, guns discharging into the air space and empty buildings around them.

"They—nuts?" Rubenstein stammered, his voice and look filled with astonishment.

"Maybe desperate's a better word—like I said, it's somethin' to do—isn't it?" Rourke wheeled his bike and gunned the engine back down the street, slowing at the corner, balancing the bike as he scanned the street in both directions, Rubenstein beside him again.

"Can't go back the way we came—look," and Rourke pointed in the direction leading out of the city. "Either another mob or part of the same one," he commented.

"But there's a gunfight down the other way by the border."

"Maybe they won't notice us," Rourke said—smiling, then started the Harley under him into the street, Rubenstein beside him on his left. Rourke cruised slowly over the pavement, guiding his bike around stray bricks and rocks and broken glass, cutting all the way left to avoid a pool of stagnant water swamping the right gutter and overflowing into the street. Rourke and Rubenstein rounded the corner, Rourke pulling to a halt in the middle of the street. He glanced behind him—the sound of the mob was barely audible now over the sound of the gunfire ahead, but already Rourke could see the first phalanxes of the mob behind him coming into the street which they'd just left. Ahead was the main border crossing into Juarez—and from across the river Rourke could hear gunfire as well, see the smoke of buildings afire there.

"Is this what's left of the world—my God!" Rubenstein exclaimed.

"It may sound like some kind of put-on," Rourke said slowly, "but I expected worse. And don't worry who you shoot at—they'll all be shooting at us—kind of like a diversion for them. Let's ride," and Rourke gunned his motorcycle, glancing back over his shoulder toward Rubenstein. Already, Rourke's fist was curled around the pistol grip of the CAR-15 slung under his shoulder.

Chapter Nine

Rubenstein jerked back the bolt on the Schmeisser 9mm submachine gun, checked the safety and gunned his motorcycle ahead, John Rourke's tall lean frame bent over the big Harley Davidson already several yards ahead of him. With the back of his hand, Rubenstein pushed his wire-rimmed glasses up off the bridge of his nose, bending low over his handlebars, his sparse black hair whipping across his smooth sunburnt forehead. He repeated to himself what Rourke had told him—"Don't fire that thing like it's a garden hose, practice trigger control." Rubenstein had asked what the spare magazines were for. Rourke had simply told him to sit on his motorcycle, hold the handlebars with one hand and the MP-40 subgun with the other. Then Rourke had reached over and pulled out the magazine. He'd stuck it in the saddlebag on the right side of the bike and said, "Okay—without taking that hand off the handlebar and without dropping the gun, reload."

Rubenstein had tried for a few moments, then

looked at Rourke in exasperation. "That's why," Rourke had said, "you need more than one gun, and that's why with all your guns you only fire at something, not just to make noise. And with a full-auto weapon like that you confine yourself to three-shot bursts." Rubenstein had mimicked Rourke then: "I know—practice trigger control—right?"

And now, as Rubenstein rounded a curve in the street, watching the armed men huddled along the supports for the bridge leading into Mexico and the other armed men across the wide square in building doorways and smashed-out windows, he repeated to himself, "Trigger control . . . trigger control."

The speedometer on his bike was only hovering around thirty or thirty-five, he noticed, but as he caught sight of the street beneath him, the pavement seeming to race past, it seemed as though he were doing a hundred or better. Rourke was already firing his CAR-15. It looked to Rubenstein like a long-barreled space gun with the scope mounted on the carrying handle and the stock retracted—like a ray gun in a movie about outer space.

As Rubenstein reached the middle of the square, gunfire started raining down toward him and he leveled the Schmeisser at the closest group of shooters and fired back, repeating aloud at the top of his voice so he could hear himself over the noise of the shots, "Trigger control . . . trigger control . . . trigger—"

Chapter Ten

Rourke worked the CAR-15's trigger steadily, aiming rather than at single targets at groups of targets, figuring to up his chances of making each shot count. As best he could make out as he sped along the gauntlet of armed men on each side of him, the ones by the bridge—there was a large hole in the middle of it—were Mexican, firing at Texans on the street side and also caught in a crossfire between the Texans and some other group at the far end of the bridge on the Juarez side. A man from the Mexican group started running into the street toward Rourke, what Rourke identified as a vintage Thompson SMG in his hands, spitting fire. Rourke swerved his bike, a burst of the heavy .45 ACP slugs from the tommy gun chewing into the pavement beside him. Fighting to control the bike and still keep shooting, Rourke swerved back right, his bike now less than a dozen feet from the man with the Thompson.

As the man turned to fire another burst, Rourke pumped two rounds from the semiautomatic Colt

CAR-15 that he held like a pistol in his fist. Both Rourke's shots slammed hard into the tommy-gun-armed man's chest, hammering him back onto the pavement. Rourke's bike skidded as the subgunner fell uncharacteristically forward, the body vaulting toward the front wheel of Rourke's bike. The bike slipped and Rourke rolled away. Flat on the street, Rourke hauled himself up to his knees and holding the CAR-15 at waist level, fired rapid, two-round semiautomatic bursts into the closest of the armed men. At the corner of his eye, Rourke could see Rubenstein, hear him shouting, "I'm coming, John!"

Rourke hauled himself to his feet. Firing the CAR-15 one-handed again like a long-barreled pistol, Rourke ran toward his bike. Two men with riot shotguns were opening up on him, running for him, Rourke guessed in order to steal the bike and his weapons. Dropping to one knee, he swapped the CAR-15 into his left hand, firing it empty at the two attackers, and snatching the Python from the leather on his right hip, he fired it as well.

Backstepping, holstering the Python and making a rapid magazine change on the CAR-15, Rourke hauled his bike up, kicked it started and let the CAR-15 hang at his side on its black web sling as he started the bike back into the middle of the street.

Already, more than a half-dozen men from the building side of the street were running toward him, assault rifles and pistols blazing in their hands. Swerving to avoid the fusillade of gunfire, Rourke cut back along the street, catching sight of Rubenstein coming up fast behind him. Rourke gunned his bike and jumped the curb, heading down along the sidewalk, the Mexicans there on the bridge side parting in waves before him as he bent low over his bike, firing the CAR-15. Behind him, Rourke could hear the steady, light three-round bursts of Rubenstein's German MP-40 9mm, hear Rubenstein's counterfeit Rebel yell—"Ya-hoo!"

Rourke fired the CAR-15 empty as he reached the end of the sidewalk, jumped the bike down the curb and into the street. Glancing over his shoulder, he could see Rubenstein close behind him, the "Schmeisser" shot empty, the Browning High Power firing from his hand as he jumped the sidewalk and into the street. Rourke heard the rebel yell again as the noise of the gunfire died in the background behind him. Under his breath, bending low over his bike, Rourke muttered, "That kid's really gettin' into it."

Chapter Eleven

Major Vladmir Karamatsov glanced to Captain Natalia Tiemerovna at his side in the gathering darkness. He could just make out the outline of her profile, the skin of her face smudged with black camouflage stick, a black silk bandanna tied over her hair, her hands fitted with tight black leather fingerless gloves, a close-fitting black jumpsuit covering the rest of her lithe body. He noticed her hands again—she held an assault rifle the way most women held a baby, he noted. A smile crossed his thin lips, his black camouflage-painted cheeks creasing at the corners of his mouth into heavy lines.

Karamatsov upped the safety catch on the blued-black Smith & Wesson Model 59 in his right hand. Like all the people in his special KGB liquidation squad, he carried strictly American or Western European-made firearms. In the event that they encountered a substantial American force, regular or irregular, there was nothing to identify himself or any of his handpicked, personally trained team as

Soviet—their English was perfect midwestern, all of them trained, as was Karamatsov himself, at the KGB's top-secret "Chicago" espionage school. They had read American books and newspapers, watched videotapes of American television, worn American-made clothes, trained on American-made firearms. American food, American slang—everything so American that they soon thought, talked and acted like Americans who had lived in America all their lives—with the one exception being their often-tested allegiance to the KGB.

Like most of the top clandestine operatives in the KGB, Karamatsov—like the girl beside him in the darkness—had gone to the Chicago school in his mid-teens. He had grown up playing basketball and betting on the World Series. For years, Karamatsov's one outside interest besides chess had been American football. He had arranged to attend three Super Bowls and had sat in the crowd happily munching hot dogs, drinking beer and shouting and cheering no less earnestly than everyone around him. He had been Arnold Warshawski of South Bend, Indiana, or Craig Bates of Milwaukee, Wisconsin, or someone else. Karamatsov was a past master at dying his hair, creating life-mask wrinkles or built-up noses. Sometimes he would stroke his cheek expecting to find a full beard and remember suddenly that that had been yesterday—instead of forty-three with a red beard and broken nose he was twenty-eight with blond hair, a small mustache and a nose that looked as though it had been the model for a Roman or Greek statue.

And very frequently over the years he had worked with the magnificent Natalia—sometimes they had posed as husband and wife, sometimes as brother and sister, sometimes as father and daughter. He liked her best as she looked now, the black hair just past the shoulders, her own strikingly dark blue eyes rather than contacts which had made them appear brown or green, her own slightly upturned nose—the figure that he had warmed himself beside so many nights. She was technically his second-in-command, his right hand. Her heart was too soft, sometimes, he reflected; but it had never interfered with her work.

He stared into the darkness, trying to make out the shapes of the others of his team who were there—Nicolai, Yuri, Boris, Constantine . . . he could not see them and Karamatsov smiled because of this.

His head itched under the black watch cap he wore. He scratched the itch, checked the Rolex watch on his wrist and felt again in the darkness the safety catch on the fifteen-shot 9mm pistol he held, checked the position of the tiny blue Chiefs Special .38 in the small of his back, checked the 9mm MAC-10 slung from his shoulder.

He watched the face of the Rolex, and as the hand swept into position, he raised up from his low crouch and started into a dead run, Natalia—as she always was, he thought comfortably—beside him, ready to die for him. The ranch house was just beyond the end of the bracken and as he reached the clearing, he could see the others of the team breaking from the shadows as well.

There was gunfire coming from the house, slow as though from a bolt action rifle. A shotgun went off in the darkness—none of his men carried a shotgun and he cursed. He kept on running, the pistol raised in his hand, 9mm slugs—115-grain jacketed hollow points—spinning from its muzzle toward the plate glass front of the building. He could hear glass shattering. There was a faster-working rifle now firing into his team in the darkness, and he tried to make out the sound. As he turned to bear his pistol down onto the suspected target, he turned to his left and saw Natalia, down on one knee, the H-K assault rifle to her shoulder, firing steady three-shot bursts, the window that had been Karamatsov's projected target shattering and even in the near total darkness the ill-defined shape of a body falling forward through the glass and into the bed of white flowers just outside.

Karamatsov started running again, first to reach the front door, kicking at the lock, which held, then stepping back and blasting at it with the MAC-11 on full auto. Natalia was beside him, her left foot smashing toward the lock, kicking the shot-through mechanism away, swinging the door inward. Karamatsov rolled through.

The house was in near total darkness. He fired the MAC-11 at a flash of brightness, his gun going empty on him. Rather than swapping magazines, he reached for the Model 59 pistol—he gauged there were at least eight rounds left in it.

There was another flash in the darkness and he fired twice, hearing a moaning sound then a heavy thud as there was another gunshot, the fireburst of the muzzle going off in the direction of the ceiling.

He stood in a crouch, his fists wrapped around the

pistol butt, the first finger of his right hand poised against the revolverlike trigger of the auto-loading pistol.

He could hear the rustle of Natalia's clothes as she moved through the darkness.

"There is no electric power here, Vladmir."

"Lights—and on guard," Karamatsov shouted. There was a clicking sound, followed immediately by a second similar sound and suddenly the room was bathed in light. He glanced obliquely at the powerful lanterns now in the middle of the floor, staying out of the circle of light to guard against still another defender being alive somewhere in the house.

"I don't think Chambers is here—President Chambers," Natalia added as an afterthought and walked toward Karamatsov, standing beside and a little behind him, the H-K in her hands, its muzzle moving like a wand through the darkness.

Karamatsov put his arm around her shoulders, whispering, "As always—you are my right arm, Natalia."

Then Karamatsov moved away from her, issuing orders to the men standing on the edge of the wall of darkness.

Chapter Twelve

Natalia Anastasia Tiemerovna moved through the darkness toward what she perceived as the outline of a staircase. "I'm searching upstairs," she declared, then added, "Yuri—back me up," glanced over her shoulder—her eyes were becoming accustomed to the darkness—and saw the blonde-haired Yuri a few steps behind her, the dark mass of a pistol in his right hand. "Sure thing, little lady," he said. She disliked the Texas-style accent Yuri had trained in recently. She turned, glaring at him, hoping somehow that even in the darkness she could signal her displeasure.

She witnessed his shrug, then she turned back toward the stairs and took them two at a time, the stock on her H-K collapsed, the .308 calibre selective fire assault rifle held at her hip like a submachine gun.

She reached the top of the stairs and stopped against the wall, flat, buttocks and shoulder blades against it, listening. She pulled the black silk bandanna from her hair and shook her head, stuffing the scarf in the front of her jumpsuit. Balling her fists around the rifle, she turned in one fluid motion into the hallway, the H-K's muzzle sweeping the open space.

"Check the rooms on the left," she commanded to Yuri, then without waiting for a response started to examine the first room on the right. The door was open halfway and she kicked it in, dodging inside and across the doorframe, going into a crouch, the H-K's selector on auto, her finger poised against the trigger.

Nothing.

She left the room and went into the hallway. One other room remained on the right—the side facing the front yard. She was almost certain there had been someone there with a rifle as they had stormed the house. The door was closed.

She stopped in front of it, took a half-step back and kicked it in, firing the H-K in rapid three-shot bursts as she sidestepped away from the doorway and into the room. She could hear breathing there in the darkness to her left, heard a brief flurry of movement and opened fire, two three-shot bursts. There was a heavy groaning sound and the dull thud of a body hitting the floor.

She mentally flipped a coin, then, holding the H-K in her right hand by the pistol grip, took the small Tekna light from her waist and twisted it on awkwardly one-handed, flashing its beam in the direction of the noise. There was a man on the floor, eyes opened, a lever-action Winchester in his hands—he was dead. "Not Chambers," she whispered to herself. The man was Latino—a Mexican ranch-worker, she theorized, one of many thousands she had been taught were exploited by the capitalists for long hours and short wages. She looked at the dead man once again, regretting his death and pitying him for having died defending his exploiters against those who would liberate him from his chains.

She turned and left the room, brushing a stray lock of hair from her forehead with the back of her still gloved left hand.

Chapter Thirteen

Very slowly, Sarah Rourke climbed back up the slope and out of the valley. At the back of her mind, she knew she couldn't leave Ron Jenkins' body on the street in the town below—there were packs of dogs running the hills and mountains now and his body might well be partially devoured by morning. She was tired, at the prospect of burying Ron Jenkins and from the added weight of his pistol and rifle. The pistol was a gun like the one she carried in the waistband of her Levis, a .45 Colt Automatic, but smaller than her husband's gun and having a differently shaped hammer. She had no idea what kind of rifle Jenkins had carried, but it was heavy, she decided, as she reached the top of the rise and turned through the darkness toward their camp, her breath short.

It was as though she had never left, she thought. Michael was sitting up with Annie's head on his lap. Carla Jenkins was sitting stock straight on the ground a few feet away from him, staring blankly into the darkness, her daughter Millie cradled in her arms. Sarah Rourke walked toward Carla Jenkins, dropped to her knees on the ground beside the woman and said nothing. Carla turned, even in the darkness the frightened set of her eyes unmistakable to Sarah Rourke.

"That's Ron's rifle—and you got his pistol belt there, too," she said softly.

"Carla—I don't. I, ah . . . I don't know how to tell you—"

"He is dead," Carla Jenkins said flatly.

"Yes," Sarah murmured.

"I'd like to be alone for a few minutes, Sarah. Can you take care of Millie for me?"

Sarah nodded, then realized that in the darkness Carla Jenkins might not have understood and said, "Of course I will, Carla." The Jenkins woman handed the ten-year-old girl into Sarah Rourke's arms and Sarah, leaving Jenkins' guns beside Carla, walked the few feet toward her own children. She dropped to her knees, trying to get into a sitting position.

She turned her head before she realized why—a gunshot, she realized. Putting Millie down on the ground, Sarah half crawled, half ran the few feet to Carla Jenkins. Sarah reached down to the Jenkins woman's head there on the ground by her feet. Her hand came away wet and slightly sticky. "Can you take care of Millie for me?" Sarah had told Carla, "Of course I will."

"Ohh, Jesus," Sarah Rourke cried, dropping to her knees beside Carla Jenkins' body, wanting to cover her own face with her hands but sitting on her haunches instead, perfectly erect, the bloody right hand held away from her body at arms' length. . . .

Sarah Rourke couldn't load Carla Jenkins' body across the saddle without getting her son, Michael, to help—and the thought of asking him had revolted her more than manhandling the body, but he had done it, simply asking her why Mrs. Jenkins had shot herself. Miraculously, Millie was sleeping still, as was Annie. Sitting with Michael a few feet away, not comprehending how the girls had slept through the gunshot, she began, "Well—sometimes death is awfully hard for people to accept. Do you understand?"

"Well," he had said, knitting his brow, "maybe a little."

"No—" Sarah said, looking down into the darkness and then back at her son's face. "See, if all of a sudden on Saturday morning—before the war—I had told you that you couldn't watch any cartoon shows at all and never explained why, told you you'd never see a cartoon show again, how would you have felt?"

"Mad."

"Sad, too?" she asked.

"Yeah. Yeah, I would have been sad."

"And probably the worst part of it making you mad and sad would have been that there wasn't any reason why—huh?"

"Yeah—I'd want to know why I couldn't watch TV."

"Well, see when Mr. Jenkins died, I guess his wife—Mrs. Jenkins—just couldn't understand why he had to die. And losing someone you love is more important than missing cartoon shows, right?"

"Yeah, I guess."

"Well, see, once somebody is dead you never get him back."

"But in church they said that after you die you live forever."

"I hope so," Sarah Rourke said quietly.

Chapter Fourteen

"I never ate something so bad in my life," Rubenstein said, starting to turn away from Rourke to spit out the food in his mouth.

"I'd eat that if I were you," Rourke said softly. "Protein, vitamins, sugar—all of that stuff, including the moisture—is something your body is craving right now. Just reading a book burns up calories, so riding that bike all day, especially in this heat, really draws a lot out of your body."

"Aww, God, but this tastes like cardboard."

"You eat much cardboard?"

"Well, no, but you know what I mean."

"It doesn't taste good, but it's nutritious. Maybe we'll find something better tomorrow or the next day. When we get back to the retreat, you can stuff yourself. I've got all the Mountain House freeze-dried foods—beef stroganoff, everything. I've got a lot of dehydrated vegetables, a freezer full of meat—steaks, roasts, the works. I've even got Michelob, pretzels, chocolate chip cookies, Seagrams Seven. Everything."

"Ohh, man—I wish we were there."

"Well," Rourke said slowly, "wishing won't get us there."

"What I wouldn't do for a candy bar—mmm. . . ."

"Unless you're under high energy demand circumstances, candy isn't that good for you. Sugar is one of the worst things in the world."

"I thought you said you had chocolate chip cookies," Rubenstein said.

"Well—you can't always eat stuff that's healthy for you."

"What kind of chocolate chip cookies are they?" Rubenstein asked.

"I don't remember," Rourke said. "I always confuse the brands."

"I found your one weakness!" Rubenstein exclaimed, starting to laugh. "Bad at identifying chocolate chip cookies."

Rourke grinned at Rubenstein, "Nobody's perfect, I guess."

Rubenstein was still laughing, then started coughing and Rourke bent toward him, saying, "Hold your hands over your head—helps to clear the air passage."

"This—pukey—damned baby—baby food," Rubenstein coughed.

"Just shut up for a minute until you get your breath," Rourke ordered. "Then let's get a few hours' rest and get started before first light again. I'd like to put on as much desert mileage as we can during darkness—want to make Van Horn and beyond tomorrow."

"What's at Van—Van Horn?" Rubenstein asked, coughing but more easily.

"Maybe food and water and gasoline. Good-sized town, a little off the beaten track, maybe it's in decent shape still. At least I hope so. Knew a guy from Van Horn once."

"Think he's still there?" Rubenstein said, speaking softly and clearing his throat.

"I don't know," Rourke said thoughtfully. "Lost touch with him a few years ago. Might have died—no way to tell."

Rubenstein just shook his head, starting to laugh again, saying, "John, you are one strange guy. I've never met somebody so laid back in my whole life."

Rourke just looked at Rubenstein, saying, "That's exactly how I'm going to be in about thirty seconds—laid back. And sleeping. You'd better do the same." Rourke stood up, starting away from the bikes.

"Takin' a leak?" Rubenstein queried.

Rourke turned and glanced back at him. "No—I'm burying the jar from the baby food. No sense littering, and the sugar clinging to the sides of the glass will just draw insects."

"Ohh," Rubenstein said.

Chapter Fifteen

Karamatsov paced across the room—dawn was coming and lighting it, drawing long shadows through the shot-open windows. "We must find Chambers—he would still be in Texas. This is his power base, and the militia units we have heard of and observed would be satisfactory troops around which he could organize armed resistance."

"Perhaps he is only hiding," Natalia observed, leaning back on one elbow on the long sofa where she had slept the remainder of the night after securing the house.

"I doubt it, Natalia. He must strike while the iron is warm—"

"Hot," she corrected.

"Yes—hot. He must, though. Once our forces are settled into position in strength his task will be more difficult. Once we are able to organize a national identity system, collect all firearms, etc., his task will be virtually impossible. He must act now!" and Karamatsov hammered his fist down on the wall behind him.

"What we gonna do, boss?" Yuri said, grinning.

Karamatsov glared at the man, but continued speaking, ignoring the lack of formality. "We are going to split up—that is what we are going to do. Natalia—you and Yuri will take an aircraft into the western portion of the state—it is desert there. Travel by jeep back to Galveston. We will all rendezvous there at our command center near the coast. Equipment and fortifications should be finished within days there at any event. Radio communications will still be impossible, so unless a perfect opportunity presents itself to get Chambers, try nothing on your own, but instead run down as many leads as possible concerning his whereabouts and anticipated movements. Questions?"

"What about identities?" Yuri's voice sounded more serious now.

"We don't have time to manufacture anything new—simply use the papers you have with you to best advantage. Unless you run into a skeptical, organized force there shouldn't be any difficulty. I wish I could offer more advice. Any other questions?"

Natalia said nothing, but uncoiled herself from the couch, standing, pressing her hands down along the sides of her coveralls. Karamatsov looked at her and watched as she ran her long fingers through her dark hair. "Natalia—I wish to speak with you a moment." Karamatsov caught Yuri's eyes glancing quickly, almost furtively at him. Natalia turned to face him and smiled, her long mouth upturned at the corners into a smile, the tiniest of dimples appearing there as if by some magic.

He turned and walked to the corner of the room, then looked back as Natalia walked toward him, the other already leaving for the front yard. "What is it, Vladmir?" she asked, the sound of her voice almost something he could feel.

"Nothing, really—I just wished to tell you to be careful. That's all. These surviving Americans are crazy. All of them with guns, so ready to use them."

"Was there anything else?" she asked, her eyes intent on his.

Karamatsov put his hands on her shoulders and drew her toward him, felt the curves of her body pressing against him. "Yes—we can be together at the headquarters. I couldn't sleep last night—do you know that?" Without waiting for her to answer, he moved his hands to her face and drew her mouth up toward his, kissing her, his hands moving down then and cradling her body against him. He bent and touched his lips to her throat, hearing her voice whispering in his ear, "Vladmir—I so want this all to be over. We can be together, now that we have won."

He held her head against his chest, his fingers stroking her hair, saying, "This is the major step that we have dreamed of, Natalia. But America is not yet conquered, our work is far from finished. But we can be together—more and more."

She looked up into his eyes and Karamatsov kissed her again.

Chapter Sixteen

Sarah Rourke wiped the dirt from her hands on the sides of her jeans, taking a step back from the large grave. She had buried both Carla and Ron Jenkins there, then, with Michael's help, gathered rocks to cover the mound by the side of the road leading into the town. Two thick branches and one of Ron Jenkins' saddle thongs had made the cross, and with Jenkins' pocket knife she had tried to scratch names on it, but only the half-rotted bark had fallen away.

"Are you all right, Michael?" she asked, looking down at her son standing beside her.

"I'm all right, Mom," the six-year-old answered, staring at the mound of dirt and stone.

She looked back over her shoulder then, saw Millie and Annie playing together by the horses and then looked back to Michael. "Do you think we should have Millie and Ann come over and help us pray for the Jenkins?"

Michael didn't answer for a moment, but then said, "No—I think they're happy playing. It might just make Millie and Annie cry again. We can pray for them ourselves."

"Maybe you're right," Sarah said. "Let's just each of us be quiet a minute and say something to ourselves, okay?"

Michael nodded and closed his eyes, knitting his dirty fingers together as though he were saying grace. As she closed her own eyes, she heard him mumbling, "God is gracious, God is good. . . ." Her eyes still closed, she reasoned it was probably the only prayer the boy knew.

Chapter Seventeen

Natalia pulled the straw cowboy hat down low over her eyes, squinting into the sun as she stood beside the jeep, waving to the departing cargo pilot. She turned her head as the dust became too intense and saw Yuri, his hair blowing in the wind the plane was generating. She held her hands to her mouth like a megaphone, shouting, "Let's get out of here!" but there was no answer, no recognition that he had even heard her. Shrugging her shoulders under the short leather jacket she wore, she climbed into the passenger seat and checked her pistol while she waited for Yuri. She had left the H-K assault rifle behind as being out of character. Yuri was supposed to be her brother and he was supposed to be a geologist. They had been out in the field—"What war?" she would say. "We were in the desert. Our radio stopped working, but we thought it was just sunspot activity or something." She looked at the gun in her hand. "Oh, this?" she would say. "Just in case of snakes. My brother showed me how it works and just insisted that I carry it but I really don't know anything about guns." She turned the gun over in her hand. Like all the American- and Western European-origin conventional guns she and the rest of Karamatsov's team used, they had been acquired technically illegally according to American law. This was a particularly nice one and she liked it, despite its limited capacity—a four-barreled stainless steel .357 Magnum COP pistol, derringerlike with a rotating firing pin and an overall size approximating a .380 automatic. It was pattern loaded, the first round intended for snakes—a .38-.357 shot shell, the last three chambers loaded with 125-grain jacketed hollow point .357s. With the gun she had a set of .22 Long Rifle insert barrels, which even more greatly expanded its versatility.

She put the gun back in the inside pocket of her leather jacket and leaned back on the seat, pulling the hat lower over her eyes, the bandanna knotted around her throat already wet with perspiration, her dark glasses doing little to reduce the harsh glare of the sun.

She turned her head, closing her eyes, when Yuri said, "Well, little lady—ya'll ready to get on with this here safari?"

She opened her eyes. "Yuri—you are a fine agent. But if you do not stop talking like that to me, you will find cyanide in your tea, or a curare-tipped straight pin inside your trouser leg. I don't like being called 'little lady.' You are not to call me Captain Tiemerovna in the field. You are to call me Natalie, the American way of saying my first name. I should not call you Yuri—why are you not correcting me?

Your name for this operation is Grady Burns. I will call you that."

Yuri looked at her, running his fingers through his hair, pulling his hat down low over his nearly squinted-shut eyes. "Yes ma'am," he said, chōking a laugh, then cranking the key and throwing the jeep into gear.

She turned toward him, started to say something, then eased back into her seat, laughing out loud in spite of herself. "Yuri—my God."

"Now that's American—little lady!" he said, laughing, his right hand moving from the gear shift and slapping her left knee. She sat bolt upright, looked at him a moment and started laughing again. They drove, talking, joking, through the sand dunes and in the general direction of Van Horn, where they hoped to find some information regarding Chambers. At one o'clock she called a halt, telling Yuri, "I've got to stretch my legs."

He pulled the jeep to a halt, shutting off the motor. "Do you want me to get it out of the back of the jeep?"

She glared at him. "Whose idea was that chemical toilet?"

"Karamatsov's idea—I think he was looking out for your comfort."

"He needn't have bothered," she stated flatly, getting out of the jeep and walking toward a low-rising dune fifteen yards to their right.

When she finished, she buried the tissue in the sand under her heel as she zipped her fly. Automatically, she started to feel for her pistol as she started back toward the jeep, remembering then that she had left it in the pocket of her jacket still on the seat. As she turned back toward the jeep, she screamed, in spite of herself. Almost instantly regaining her composure, she shouted, "Who are you?" Two men, wearing T-shirts and faded jeans, were standing on the top of the small dune, their faces leering. "I said, who are you?"

"I heard what ya' said, girl," the taller of the two men shouted back.

She started walking again, slowly. She stopped when she saw the jeep. Two men dressed like the first two were standing beside it, and a short distance behind them were four motorcycles. She couldn't see Yuri.

She turned to the two men on the top of the dune, one of whom was already sliding down toward her. "Where is he—the man on the jeep, the man I was with?"

"Well, you don't have to worry yourself 'bout him no more—he's dead. Slit his throat just as nice as you please, we did," the nearer man told her.

She found herself shaking her head. Yuri was too good to have let himself be surprised like that. "I don't believe you," she said.

"See," the taller man began, sliding to the ground and getting to his feet less than a yard from her. "He never noticed this," and he reached into his hip pocket and flicked open a long-bladed switchblade, "'cause he was too busy lookin' at that," and the tall man gestured back toward the top of the dune. The second man swung his right hand from behind him now, a shotgun in it, the barrels impossibly short, she thought, the stock of the shotgun all but gone. She noticed a leather strap from the butt of the shotgun stretched across the man's body like a sling.

"While your boyfriend was a lookin', I was a cuttin'," the tall man said, grinning.

Natalia stared at him, assessing his build, the way he stood, searching him with her eyes for additional weapons. There was a pistol crammed between the wide black belt he wore and the sagging beerpot under the sweat-stained T-shirt. As near as she could make out, the gun was a German luger.

"What do you want?" she asked, lowering her voice.

"What do you think I want, girl?" the man laughed, starting to step toward her. The knife was still in his right hand and as he took his second step, Natalia moved, both hands going toward him, her right hand flashing upwards, the middle knuckles locked outward, impacting under his nose and smashing the bone upward into his brain. Her left hand had already found the nerve on the right side of his neck and pinched it, momentarily numbing the right arm, causing the knife to fall from his grasp. She knew he was dead and let him fall, dismissing the inferior switchblade knife and snatching the Luger from his belt as he went down. Her right thumb found the safety, her left hand slamming back the toggle in case the gun had been carried chamber empty, the trigger finger on her right hand poised for a fast squeeze as the toggle slammed forward, two rounds—9mms, she thought—slamming up at a sharp angle into the man with the sawed-off shotgun standing on top of the dune. She wheeled, a shot already echoing from behind her, a second shot—the sound registering somewhere at the back of her mind, creasing heavily into her left forearm, pitching her back into the sand on her rear end, her first shot toward the two men standing near the jeep going wild. She rolled across the sand, bullets kicking it up into her face. She fired, two rounds in a fast burst at the nearest man—he had a pistol. The last man was working a bolt action rifle, swinging the muzzle toward her. She fired once, shooting out the left eye. She automatically glanced down to the Luger's sights—the rear sight looked banged up and she attributed the eyeball shot to that. She had aimed between the eyes.

She started to her feet, took a step forward and fell into the sand. She rolled onto her back, the sun, still almost directly overhead, momentarily blinding her despite the sunglasses. But then she remembered she'd lost them rolling through the sand. She tried standing, felt her head—it hurt badly. Forcing herself to her feet, she staggered toward the jeep and fell against it, burning her fingers on the hot metal, the Luger slipping from her right hand. Pulling herself into the jeep and across the passenger seat, her blue eyes glanced downward—Yuri, his throat slit ear-to-ear—in a clumsy fashion, she thought—lay in the sand, his eyes wide open and staring into the sun. She started the jeep, heard a high-pitched whistle and saw steam rising from in front of the hood.

"Shot the radiator—stupid," she murmured to herself, then fumbled off the emergency brake and threw the car into gear. The thought that drove her was that the four men were probably not alone. The sketchy intelligence from the area indicated a large and heavily armed gang of looters and killers moving across the state. "Outriders," she said dully as she started the jeep up a low dune. "Got to hurry. . . ."

Chapter Eighteen

"Wait here in case it's a trap of some kind," Rourke said.

"What do you mean—a trap?" Rubenstein asked.

Rourke looked at him a moment. "Could be those paramilitary guys, could be anyone—put a woman's body down beside the road, most people are going to stop, right? Plenty of cover back by those dunes, right?"

"Yeah, but—she's awful still. Hasn't moved since we spotted her."

"Could be dead already, maybe just a bag of rags stuffed into some old clothes. Keep me covered," Rourke almost whispered. He swung the CAR-15 across the front of the Harley and started the bike slowly across the road, throwing a glance back over his shoulder, seeing Rubenstein readying the German MP-40 subgun to back him up. Rourke cut a wide arc across the opposite shoulder, going off onto the sand and running a circle around the body—it was a woman, dark hair covering half her face, her right hand clutched to her left arm, dark bloodstains seeping through her fingers. Rourke stopped the bike a few yards from her, dismounted and kept the CAR-15 pointed in her general direction, his right fist bunched around the pistol grip, his first finger just outside the trigger guard.

He walked slowly across the sand, the sun to his left now starting to sink rapidly, because, technically—despite the heat—it wasn't quite spring. Darkness would come soon, and Van Horn was still miles away. Water and food were virtually gone—and, of more immediate concern, so was the gasoline. His bike was nearly empty and he doubted Rubenstein's bike would make even another twenty or thirty miles.

He stopped, staring at the woman's body inches from the dusty toes of his black combat boots. Rourke pushed the sunglasses back from his head and up into his hair, staring at her more closely. She was incredibly beautiful, even dirty and disheveled as she was now, and somewhere at the back of his mind Rourke knew he'd seen the face before. "I wouldn't forget you," he murmured, then pushed the toe of his left boot toward her, moving her body a little and finally rolling her over. The limpness of her body spelled recent death or a deep state of unconsciousness. He dropped to one knee beside her, swinging the scoped CAR-15 behind his back, bending down to her then and taking her head gently into his left hand, his right thumb slowly opening her left eyelid. She was alive. He felt her pulse, weak but steady. Her skin was waxy-appearing and cold to the touch. "Shock," he murmured to himself. "Heat prostration." Rourke looked up and called across the road.

"Paul—do a wide circle to make sure she doesn't have any friends, then come over—we've got to get her out of the sun."

Rourke scanned the horizon to see if there were any natural shade, fearing she might not survive until darkness. About a hundred yards off to the opposite side of the road, he spotted an overhanging outcropping of bare rock. Quickly feeling the woman's arms and legs and along the rib case to ascertain that there were no readily apparent broken bones, he stood up, bringing the unconscious girl to her feet, then sweeping her up into his arms. As Rubenstein completed his circuit and drove up alongside, Rourke, the girl cradled in his arms like a child, said, "I'm heading over toward those rocks on the other side of the road. Bring your bike over there, then come back for mine." Rourke didn't wait for an answer, but started across the concrete, his knees slightly flexed under the added weight of the girl in his arms. As he reached the opposite shoulder he looked down, felt her stirring there. She was moving her lips. ". . . find Sam Chambers . . . get to jeep," and she repeated herself, over and over again as Rourke reached the shelter of the rocks with her. The sun low, there was ample shade. Rourke set her down in the sand as gently as he could. Rubenstein was already coming back with Rourke's Harley. Rourke looked up as Rubenstein ground to a dusty halt. "We've got to normalize her body temperature. Get me the water—she needs it more than we do."

Rourke looked down at the girl's face. He nodded to himself. It was a face he wouldn't forget and he remembered it now but couldn't yet make the connection.

Chapter Nineteen

The moon was bright but there was a haze around it—Sarah Rourke recalled her husband using the phrase "blood on the moon." There was enough blood on the earth, she thought. All through the day she had followed along the path of the brigands who had tortured Ron Jenkins and everywhere they had gone—small farms, two more towns—the scene had been the same. Wanton destruction and dead people and animals everywhere. But their trail had taken a sharp turn back into the northeastern portion of the state and now, as she guessed she was crossing the border into Tennessee, as best as she could judge they were behind her and going in an entirely different direction, each mile taking them farther apart.

She pulled up on the reins. Tildie slowed and stopped, bending her head down low and browsing the ground. Sarah Rourke looked behind her. Michael was riding her husband's horse Sam by himself now, and Millie and her own daughter Annie were riding Carla Jenkins' mount and Ron Jenkins' appaloosa was carrying most of the cargo. It was a better arrangement for the animals, and every few hours she swapped horses with Michael to rest Tildie from her weight. It would be several more days before they reached Mt. Eagle, Tennessee and tried searching for Millie's aunt who had a small farm there. Earlier in the day, Sarah had tried questioning Millie about where the farm was, but the girl had remained silent, just as she had been since the death of her parents the previous night. At the back of her mind, Sarah Rourke realized that if the girl did not respond, trying to find her surviving family would be hopeless. And by leaving Georgia, Sarah thought bitterly, she was cutting down on her own chances of reuniting with her husband. She had concretized the idea in her mind that John Thomas Rourke was still alive, out there somewhere and looking for her even now. She realized that if she once abandoned that idea she would be without hope.

She could not see any value in a life of constantly running from outlaws or brigands, living in the wild like hunted animals. She bent low over the saddle horn. The pains in her stomach were increasing in frequency and severity. It wasn't the time of the month for her period, though she supposed it possible she was having it early. But the cramps were somehow different anyway. She had tried the water near the one town they had passed, she recalled. Something had been odd-tasting and she had kept the children and the horses from it and gone on. Hours later, she had found bottled water in an abandoned convenience store and stocked up.

She turned quickly when she heard a noise from

one of the horses behind her. It was Sam—her husband's horse. As she started to turn her head back, she doubled over the saddle, gagging, her head suddenly light and hurting badly. She started to dismount but couldn't straighten up, tumbling from the saddle onto her knees on the ground.

"Momma!"

"Mommie!" The last voice was Annie's. Sarah started to push herself to her feet, wanting to say something to Michael. She pulled on the base of the left stirrup near her hand, but as she stood she slumped against the saddle, colored lights in her eyes. She could feel the blood rushing to her head. Her hands slipped from the saddle horn and she tried grabbing at the stirrup but couldn't. . . .

Chapter Twenty

Rubenstein sat in the darkness, watching the rising and falling of the strange girl's chest in the moonlight, listening to her heavy breathing, the Schmeisser cradled in his lap. His mouth was dry. He'd given up cigarette smoking two years earlier, but now having a cigarette was all he could think about. He looked at the Timex on his wrist. Rourke had been gone for more than an hour. "That woman keeps mumbling about a jeep," Rourke had said. "If there is one out there, that should mean food and water, maybe gasoline."

"But she wouldn't have left it if it hadn't been out of gas," Rubenstein had countered.

"People out here in the desert don't usually let themselves run out of gas. Could have punched a hole in a radiator, severed a fuel line. Could still be enough gas to run these bikes into Van Horn. Otherwise, we've got a long walk ahead of us and we used our last water with her."

"You're the survivalist, the expert," Rubenstein

had said, almost defensively. "Can't you just go out there and find water?"

"Yeah," Rourke had answered. "If I take a hell of a long time doing it I can, and I can find us food, too—but not gasoline. Even if I discovered crude oil it wouldn't do us any good."

And Rourke had mounted up and gone, leaving the Steyr-Mannlicher SSG rifle with Rubenstein for added protection, the light-gathering qualities of the 3-9 variable Mannlicher scope that rode it something Rourke had labeled "potentially useful" if whoever had wounded the girl were still out there somewhere in the darkness. The thought of more violence-prone thieves didn't appeal to Rubenstein. He shivered in the darkness. The girl's body temperature was about normal, Rourke had said, and she wasn't really so much unconscious anymore as just sleeping. Rourke had cleansed and bandaged the deep flesh wound on her left forearm. Her right hand still had blood on it, but only blood from the arm wound, which Rourke had not washed away because of the water shortage.

Rubenstein shifted his position on the ground, hearing something in the darkness to his left. He turned and peered into the black, seeing nothing. He heard the sound again, pulling open the bolt on the Schmeisser, ready, his voice a loud whisper, saying, "I know you're out there—I hear you. I've got a sub-machine gun, so don't try anything."

"That doesn't do much to scare a rattler, Paul," Rourke said softly. Rubenstein wheeled, seeing Rourke standing beside the sleeping woman, the CAR-15 in his hands, the sling suspending the gun beneath his right shoulder. "Rattler—your body heat is drawing him. Move over."

Rubenstein took a step left. Rourke raised the CAR-15 from its carry position, drawing out the collapsible stock and bringing the rifle to his shoulder. "What are you doing?" Rubenstein said.

"I'm sighting with the iron—this kind of scope wouldn't be much good at this range."

Rourke shifted his feet, settling the rifle, and suddenly Rubenstein jumped, as Rourke almost whispered, "Bang!" then brought the rifle down and collapsed the stock.

"Bang?"

"Yeah—If I shoot that snake—unless he comes into camp and we have to, all I'm going to do is advertise to everybody and his brother we're here, we've got guns and we're stupid enough to go shooting at something in the dark. Keep an eye out for that snake and I'll bring my bike up."

"Why did you leave it?"

"What if something had happened, somebody'd wandered into camp and gotten the drop on you?"

"That wouldn't have happened," Rubenstein insisted, his voice sounding almost hurt.

"Happened to her," Rourke said slowly. "After I found her jeep, I backtracked it. I didn't figure I'd have to go far. There was a bullet hole in the radiator and in today's heat the thing couldn't have gone far without the engine stalling out. Dead man. Either her boyfriend or her husband and they just didn't believe in rings. Throat slit ear to ear. Four other dead men there—bikers, well armed. Looks like our ladyfriend there shot all four but one of them."

"Maybe the other one's still out there," Rubenstein said.

"No condition to do anything to us—looks like she broke his nose and drove the bone up into his brain. Professional young lady. I found a jacket that looked like it was small enough to be hers—had an interesting little gun in it. The dead man with his throat slit was carrying a Walther P-38K. Pretty professional piece of hardware—the muzzle was threaded on the inside for a silencer. I found the silencer back at the jeep stuffed inside one of the tubular supports for the seat frame."

"Jesus," Rubenstein exclaimed.

"I don't think that was his name," Rourke said quietly, turning then and fading back into the darkness.

Chapter Twenty-One

Michael Rourke opened his dark eyes, squinting against the sun. His legs ached and he started to move, but then remembered the weight on his lap. He looked down at his mother's face, the eyes still closed. "Momma," he said softly. "Wake up—it's morning."

He looked across the flat expanse of ground and confirmed the rising sun. Millie and Annie were still asleep. The horses were still tied to the tree that he'd secured the reins to the previous night. Their saddles were still in position. After his mother had fallen down and he hadn't been able to waken her, he'd had Millie and Annie watch her and he had loosened the straps under the horses' bellies that held the saddles on—his mother called them "cinches," he remembered.

"Momma," he said again, shaking her head gently. He closed his eyes. "Millie, Annie! Get up—time to get up!" he shouted. Annie sat bolt upright, stared around her and then at him.

"How is Mommie?" she said.

"She'll be okay," he said. "Wake up Millie and have her make something to eat. You know where it is—the food. Millie can reach the bags."

He looked back to his mother. The sunlight was just hitting her face and he watched her eyelids moving. "Momma!"

Sarah Rourke opened her eyes. "Ohh," she started, her voice sounding hoarse to him.

"Annie—get Momma some water."

Sarah Rourke stared at him—Michael couldn't tell if she was all right or not.

"Momma—are you going to be okay?"

He saw her moving her right hand toward him and he bent toward her, felt her hand—cold—against his cheek. "Momma!"

"Shh," Sarah said, the corners of her mouth raising faintly in a smile. "I'll be all right—just give me a hug and don't ask me to get up for a while—okay?"

Chapter Twenty-Two

Rourke stepped away from the low yellow campfire and sat back against the rock face, staring out across the desert as the sun—orange against a gray sky—winked up over the horizon to the east. He hunched his shoulders in his leather jacket, both hands wrapped around a white-flecked black metal mug of steaming coffee.

He glanced at Rubenstein when the younger man spoke, "Now this is more like it—life on the trail, I mean. Food, coffee, water. Hey—" and Rubenstein leaned back against the far end of the rocks.

"Simple things can mean a lot," Rourke observed, staring then at the woman, still sleeping when last he'd looked, lying on a ground cloth between them. Her eyelids were starting to flutter, then opened and she started to sit up, then fell back.

"Give yourself a few minutes," Rourke said slowly to her.

"What's that I smell?" she said, her voice hoarse.

"Coffee—want some? It's yours, anyway," Rourke

told her.

She sat up again, this time moving more slowly, leaning back on her elbow. "Who are you?" she asked, her voice still not quite right-sounding to Rourke.

"My name is John Rourke—he's Paul Rubenstein," and Rourke gestured over her. She turned and Rubenstein smiled and gave her a little salute.

"What the hell are you doing drinking my coffee?"

"Pleasant, aren't we?" Rourke said. "You were dying, we saved your life. I went back and found your jeep, buried your boyfriend or husband a few miles back beyond that, hauled up the gasoline, the water, the food, some of your stuff. Then so we didn't have to leave you alone and could make sure your fever didn't come up, we slept in shifts the rest of the night watching you. I figure that earns me a cup of coffee, some gas and some food and water. Got any objections?"

"You got any cigarettes?" Natalia said. "And some coffee?"

"Here," Rourke said, tossing a half-empty pack of cigarettes to her. "I guess these are yours—found 'em at the jeep." She started to reach out her left arm for the cigarettes and winced.

"You were shot in the forearm," Rourke commented, then looked back to his coffee, sipping at it.

"Anybody got a light?"

Rourke reached into his jeans and pulled out his Zippo, leaning across to her and working the wheel, the blue-yellow flame leaping up and flickering in the wind. The girl looked at him across it, their eyes meeting, then she bent her head, brushing the hair back. The tip of the cigarette lighted orange for a moment, then a cloud of gray smoke issued from her mouth and nostrils as she cocked her head back, staring up at the sky.

"I agree—but I'd already noticed you're beautiful," Rourke said deliberately.

She turned and looked at him, laughing, saying, "I think I know you from somewhere—I mean that should be your line, but I really do. That bandage is very professional."

Rubenstein said, "John's a doctor—among other things."

Rourke glanced across at Rubenstein, saying nothing, then looked at the girl. "I had the same feeling when I first saw you by the road, that I know you from somewhere."

"What happened?"

"I was hoping you could tell me. Paul and I just spotted your body by the side of the road, saw you were hurt and tried to help."

"Did I talk—I mean how did you know where to find the jeep?"

"You didn't say much," Rourke said, adding, "Don't worry. You mumbled something about a jeep and something about Sam Chambers. If I remember, before the war he was still down here in Texas—just been appointed secretary of communications to the president."

"The war?" Natalia said.

"Don't you know about the war?" Rubenstein said, leaning toward her.

"What war?" Natalia said.

"Tell her about the war," Rourke said, lighting one of the last of his cigars. "Looks like it's going to rain today."

Chapter Twenty-Three

"God, it's so green here," Samuel Chambers said, sitting on the small stone bench and looking at the profusion of camelias.

"East Texas by the Louisiana border here is green like this most of the time. But I think it's time for the meeting to start now—Mr. President."

Chambers looked at the man, saying quickly, "Don't call me that yet, George. I'm secretary of communications, and that's it."

"But you're the only surviving man in the line of succession, sir—you are the president."

"I was up in Tyler last year in October for the Rose Festival—this just might be the prettiest part of the State of Texas—here, north of here and down south to the Gulf."

"Sir!"

"I'm coming, George—stop and smell the flowers, right?" Chambers stood up and reached into his shirt pocket, snatching a Pall Mall. He stared at the cigarette a moment, then said to his young executive assistant. "I wonder how I'll get these now—with the war?"

"I'm sure we can find enough to last a long time for you, sir," the young man Chambers had called George said reassuringly, walking toward Chambers and standing at his side as he passed, almost as if to keep the man from taking another tour of the garden.

Chambers turned as he reached the double french doors leading back from the walled garden to the library inside the nearly century-old stone house. He stared back into the garden, saying to George without looking at him, "I'm about to make history, George. When I walk into that room, if I reject the call to the presidency or if I accept it. And if I accept it, what will I be president of? It's a wasteland out there beyond this garden—much of it is, isn't it?"

"Yes, sir."

"Pretty much of the whole West Coast is gone, New York was blown off the map. What am I going to be offered the presidency of—a sore that isn't smart enough to know that it can't heal?"

Chapter Twenty-Four

"Who are they, John?" Rourke heard Rubenstein asking. Rourke didn't answer, staring up the road at the stricken faces of the men, women and children struggling slowly toward them. As the women's faces showed recognition of Rourke, Rubenstein and the girl bending over their cycles, Rourke watched the women hug the children closer to them, some of the men starting to raise sticks or axes as if for defense. "Who are they?" Rubenstein asked again.

Rourke turned and started to answer, but then the woman's alto, choked-sounding as she spoke, came from behind him on the Harley's long seat. "They're refugees from some town up ahead—it's written all over their faces, Paul."

"I do know you from somewhere," Rourke said to her.

"And I know you—I wonder what will happen when we remember from where, John?"

"I don't know," he said slowly, then stared back up the road at the faces of the people. He looked over to

Rubenstein on the bike beside him, saying, "Dismount and leave your subgun on the bike or give it to Natalie. Go tell them we don't mean them any harm."

"But how do I know they don't mean me any harm?" Rubenstein asked, starting off his bike.

"I'll cover you."

Rubenstein handed the SMG to Natalie, Rourke glancing back to her and saying, "Don't tell me you can't figure out how to use it—remember I saw the job you did back there at the jeep."

"Whatever do you mean," she said, her voice half laughing.

"Sure, lady," Rourke grunted, then watched as Rubenstein, hands outspread as though he were approaching an unfamiliar dog, walked toward the refugees.

Rourke heard Rubenstein starting to speak, "Hey look—we're good guys—don't mean you any harm, maybe we can help you."

A man started toward Rubenstein with a long-handled scythe and Rourke shouted, "Watch out!" then started to bring the Python out of the Ranger cammie holster on his pistol belt. There was a short, loud roar behind him, hot brass burning against his neck, the scythe handle was sliced in half, and Rubenstein spun on his heel, the Browning High Power in his right hand, his left hand pushing his glasses back off the bridge of his nose. Rourke glanced back to Natalie, saying, "Like I said, sure lady."

"The hell with you," Rourke heard her say, as she slid from the back of his Harley and handed him the

Schemiesser, the bolt still open, the safety on. She walked a few steps ahead of the bike, stopped and wiped the palms of her hands against her blue-jeaned thighs, shot a glance over her shoulder at Rourke, then started walking slowly toward the people, the refugees, the closest now less than a dozen feet from Paul Rubenstein.

Her voice was soft, low—the way you'd want your lover to sound, Rourke thought. "Listen to us—please," she was saying. "We don't want to hurt any of you at all—I just fired to protect my friend here. We want to help. We don't want to hurt you," and she walked into the front of the crowd, reaching out her right hand slowly and tousling the sandy hair of a boy of about ten, standing pressed against a woman Rourke assumed to be the boy's mother.

Rourke looked down to the MP-40, pulled the magazine and let the bolt kick forward, then reseated the magazine. He held the submachine gun in his left hand, dismounting the Harley-Davidson Low Rider and walking slowly, his right palm outstretched, toward Rubenstein, Natalie and the refugees. Natalie was talking again. "Where are you people from? What happened to you all?"

Rourke found himself looking at her—the way the sides of her hair were pulled back and caught up at the back of her head, her hair then falling past her shoulders slightly, the movement of her hands. He inhaled hard, bunching his right hand into a fist, stepping up beside her, saying, "She's telling you the truth—we just want to know where you are all from, what happened. I'm a doctor—maybe I can help some of you."

Rourke spun half-around, almost going for a gun—there was a woman screaming in the middle of the group, the faces on both sides of her melting away as Rourke took a step closer to her. She was on her knees, crying, holding a baby in her arms, the blanket stained dark red with blood.

Rourke walked over to her, gently touching her shoulder, handing off the Schmeisser and the CAR-15 to Natalie behind him. He dropped to his knees, slowly pulling back the blanket from the baby's face. The flesh was cold to his touch, the complexion blue-tinged. "This child is dead," Rourke said softly, dropping the blanket back over the infant's face and staring up skyward to where the woman holding the child was mumbling a prayer.

They spent several hours with the refugees, some thirty in all, Rourke doing what he could, Natalie finally getting the woman to release her dead baby, then helping Rubenstein bury the child by the side of the road. The people were from a town some fifteen miles or so up ahead, a place Rourke had never heard of. There had been a cafe and a U.S. Border Patrol Station there. Brigands had come, the woman said, starting to pick up the story then, rocking back and forth on her knees on the ground, her dirty face tear-streaked, blood on the front of her dress from the dead infant she had carried through the night.

"My Jim and I was sleepin'—he was tossin' and turnin' so much that it woke me up and I couldn't get back to sleep. I kept wonderin' if the radiation from the bombs was gonna get to us and kill my baby." She choked back a sob then, Natalie putting her arm around the woman's shoulders, the woman coughing and going on, ". . . and then I heard all this commotion. Engine noises, gunshots, screamin' and all. I thought maybe somethin' good was happenin', like maybe there were U.S. troops coming in, or the Border Patrol men had come back. I got up and looked out the window and saw them. . . ." Her voice trailed off into a whisper, then she began again. "There was maybe a couple hundred of them—all of them kinda young, some of them ridin' motorcycles, some of them in pickup trucks or jeeps. Some of our folks started runnin' out into the streets, some of the men shootin' at the strangers, but they all got shot down or run over. They started smashin' and burnin' everythin' then, stealin' everythin' like they owned the whole world or somethin'. Jim was up then and he took his rifle and ran out after them and they—" the woman stopped, crying now uncontrollably, her head sinking to her breast, Natalie wrapping the woman in her arms.

An old man, sitting on the ground beside Rourke began talking, "They took those of us they didn't kill and lined us up in the street. Just gunned down some of us for fun it looked like, raped some of the women there in the street makin' us all watch, took some of the women with 'em, looted all the houses and the couple stores we had, took every gun in town, all the food and water they could find and told us to go before they changed their minds about wastin' the bullets and just killin' us all."

Rourke looked away from the man, hearing Natalie say, "They must be up ahead of us, somewhere."

Rubenstein muttered, "I hope we get to meet them."

Rourke looked at Natalie, then at Paul Rubenstein, slowly then saying, "Chances are we'll meet up with them. Anybody see who shot that woman's baby—what he looked like?"

The woman Natalie had folded in her arms suddenly stopped crying, looking up at Rourke, saying, "I saw him. Not too tall, thin kind of and had blonde hair, curly and pretty like a girl maybe, and this little beard on the end of his chin. Carried a long, fancy-lookin' pistol—that's what he used to kill my baby, that's what he killed her with."

Rourke leaned forward to the woman, huddled there in Natalie's arms, saying slowly, deliberately, his voice almost a whisper. "I can't promise you we'll find that man, but I can promise you that if we do I'll kill him for you." Rourke started to turn away and caught Natalie's blue eyes staring at him. He didn't look away.

Chapter Twenty-Five

"You must assume the presidency sir," the green fatigue-clad air force colonel said, leaning forward in the mustard-colored overstuffed chair, his blue eyes focused tight on the lanky Samuel Chambers.

Chambers held up his left hand for silence, leaned back in the leather-covered easy chair and began to speak. "Colonel Darlington—you and everyone here urge me to essentially 'crown' myself as president of the United States—when I'm not even sure there still is a United States. According to Captain Reed's contact through army channels before the army ceased to function as a unified command, Soviet landings were anticipated in Chicago and several other major U.S. cities that were neutron-bombed. We could and probably do have thousands of Soviet troops already in the country and thousands more on the way. The worse the damage our forces did to them, the more desperate they'll be to utilize our surviving factories and natural resources to get their own country back on its feet. And what about the radiation fallout, the famine, the economic collapse we are facing now? Is there actually a country—even a world—that's going to be able to go on, even if it wants to? Answer me that colonel!" Chambers concluded.

Captain Reed leaned forward in his chair, a Sherlockian pipe—unlit—clamped in the left corner of his thin-lipped mouth. He snatched at the pipe with his left hand, pointed with the stem and said, "I've been listening to this sir, and I've reached one conclusion, and I think it should be obvious to everyone here by now. We're talking about a situation of mass confusion out there. The former president did what he had to do. Had he stayed alive, essentially trapped in his retreat, the Soviets could have used him for whatever they wanted to—with or without his cooperation. But you're different, sir." Reed leaned back, glanced briefly around the room and went on. "Your sentiments against Communism on a philosophical basis are widely known, so putting words in your mouth would be useless. They don't have you trapped in one spot—they don't know where you are. Now we can see that apparently there are people still alive, there are armed citizens out there willing to fight someone—but someone has to point them in the right direction, to channel what they're doing. Maybe that's the word. We need someone to channel the energies of the country. We need a leader and we don't have that now. And there's no one else but you, sir."

Reed sat back, glancing around the room again, then looking down to the floor as if studying the toes of his combat boots.

Colonel Darlington, after a long silence, said softly, "The captain is right—he put it better than any of us," then staring intently at Chambers, said, "Mr. President."

Chambers looked at Darlington, then at Reed and then at the others there in the room—Randan Soames, commander of the Texas Militia, volunteer paramilitary group; Federal Judge Arthur Bennington; his own aide, George Cripp.

Chambers lit a cigarette, saying through the cloud of smoke as he stared down in front of him, "Perhaps Judge Bennington could find a Bible so that he can administer the Oath. After that, gentlemen, I'll anticipate we'll be proceeding with this organizational conference well into tomorrow morning." Chambers looked up, catching the judge's eye, saying, "Arthur—whenever you're ready."

Moments later, Chambers stood in the garden, swore to protect and defend the Constitution of the United States, so help him God. His aide, George Cripp, was the first to address him afterward as "Mr. President."

Chapter Twenty-Six

Natalie had kept the four-barreled COP derringer-type pistol, giving the other guns Rourke had salvaged from the jeep and the brigands she had killed to the most likely-looking of the refugee group. Rourke, Rubenstein—by now understanding firearms reasonably well—and Natalie showed the new gun owners how to employ them. Sharing the water and food left Rourke and Rubenstein and the girl with enough to reach Van Horn and nothing more. Before parting company with the refugee party early the next morning, Rourke sent Rubenstein back down the road in the direction in which the refugee party would be traveling, to scout twenty miles ahead, then come back. The younger man, dark hair whipping across his high forehead, eyes squinted both against the sun and apparently to keep the perpetually slipping wire-rimmed glasses from falling off the bridge of his nose, returned almost exactly forty minutes later, reporting nothing up ahead for the refugees—and nothing close behind for Rourke.

Rourke, the girl he knew as Natalie sitting behind him on his bike, watched until the refugee group had straggled a hundred yards or so down the road, then turned to Rubenstein, straddling the Harley beside him. Rourke glanced at the smaller man, noting that the complexion which had been pallid only days earlier, and then red from the sun, was now starting to darken. Already, too, there was an added leanness about Rubenstein's face. Rourke exhaled slowly, saying, "Well, partner—about ready?"

Rubenstein looked at him, saying nothing, and nodded, then hurriedly pushed his glasses off the bridge of his nose. "You know, Paul," Rourke smiled, "We've gotta do something about getting those glasses fixed." Not looking at the girl behind him, Rourke said, "Hold on—I want to make some time." Rourke pushed the sleeves of his already sweat-stained light blue shirt up past his elbows, ran the long fingers of his hands back through his brown hair, then started his Low Rider, cutting a slow arc off the road shoulder and back onto the highway. A road sign a hundred yards off to his right, faded from the sunlight, read: "Van Horn—75 miles."

They rode in silence, flanking the yellow line at the center of the road. Rourke checked his speedometer, his odometer and then the Rolex wristwatch, then bored his eyes back up the road and gunned the cycle harder. They had driven for just under an hour when Rourke signaled to Rubenstein and started cutting across the right-hand lane to pull up alongside the right shoulder. Ahead of them stretched a low, bridged highway running past smokeless high chimneys, and beyond that were the faint outlines of buildings scorching under the already intense sun. Rourke glanced at his watch—the Rolex read nearly ten A.M. now. As Rubenstein pulled beside him, Rourke said quietly, "Van Horn," and gestured toward the lifeless-seeming factories and beyond.

"It looks dead," Rubenstein said, squinting against the light.

"Does," Rourke commented.

"What do we do?" It was Natalie, leaning over his shoulder.

"Well," Rourke began slowly. "We need food and water, and Rubenstein here could use some clip-on sunglasses before the glare does permanent damage to his eyes. You could probably stand some things. And we could use some more gasoline. I promised I'd get you as far as I could toward Galveston. I don't know yet whether Paul and I are going to have to go down that far to find a safe way of getting onto the other side of the Mississippi. From what I was able to judge from the air that night--the night of the war—it looked as though that entire area should be nothing but a nuclear desert. But there's no way of telling that from here—unless you know something."

He craned his neck and looked at the girl, who smiled at him, saying, "Remember, I hadn't even heard about the war until you and Paul told me?"

"Yeah, I remember that," Rourke said slowly. "I guess though it sort of strikes me as odd that you seem so good with a gun, seem to have seen refugees close up before, and that somewhere in the back of each of our minds we remember each other from somewhere.

I just thought maybe some vibrations or something might have come to you about the Mississippi Delta region."

"Sorry," the girl said, as though dismissing Rourke's remark.

"Right—sorry," Rourke echoed. "Well, since you just seem to have this mystical skill with borrowed handguns and submachine guns, when we get down into Van Horn, until we rearm you with something more than that little pea-shooter you've got, why don't you snatch my Python out of the leather here in case some shooting starts. I think if you study it for a while, you can figure out how it works. Right?"

The girl smiled again, almost whispering, "I'd imagine I can."

"Good," Rourke said softly, then turning to Rubenstein, "Paul, there's one main drag down there, probably. When we hit the town, I'll wait five minutes, you cut down along the perimeter as fast as you can, then turn into the main street and start back toward me. Those brigands who destroyed that town those refugees came from are up ahead of us somewhere. I figure they probably already attacked Van Horn, but some of them could have hung around. People like that are usually pretty loose organizationally, coming and going when they please. Keep that thing you call a Schmeisser ready, huh?"

"Gotcha," Rubenstein said, swinging the submachine gun off his back and slinging it under his arm.

Rourke turned back to the girl. "That Python of mine is Mag-Na-Ported—gas-venting slots on each side of the barrel. So it won't give you as much felt recoil as you might expect."

"I don't understand," the girl said.

He turned his head and looked at her a moment, saying, "Just fake it," a smile crossing his lips.

He started the Harley Davison Low Rider between his legs into first and back onto the highway and toward the bridge. The buildings coming up on his right were gray factory smokestacks from light industry. Rourke's Harley was halfway across the bridge now, and from the elevation he could look beyond the largely flat rooflines and into the town and beyond that into the gray-seeming desert. There was no sign of life. The winds were coming strong and Rourke tacked the Harley into them to keep their buffeting effect from flipping the big bike down. Three-quarters of the way across the bridge he angled right, trying to keep quartering into the wind as he did, heading the bike down and onto the off ramp into the town. Rubenstein, behind him as he looked back, was evidently having greater problems handling the heavy winds.

As Rourke's Harley dipped below the level of the bridge, the bridge itself seemed to block the winds and he swerved slightly left, then straightened out, coming to a slow halt at the base of the ramp, then cutting a lazy figure eight in the street fronting it as he scouted in both directions, then heading right from the direction he'd come and into the town itself. The main street seemed some two blocks ahead, Rourke gauged, and he waved Rubenstein down along a narrow side street, glancing over his shoulder, watching the younger man sharply turning the bike and disappearing behind an intact but deserted-appearing building.

Rourke reached the main street, slowed and cut a gentle arc in the large intersection there and came to a stop. "It looks like everyone just vanished," Natalie commented.

"I've got a bad feeling about this place," Rourke said, staring down the street, waiting to see Rubenstein reappear approximately a half-mile down.

"A Neutron bomb?" the girl asked, her voice hushed.

"Now what would a nice young lady like you know about Neutron bombs?" Rourke said, not looking at her. He settled his sunglasses and pulled back the bolt-charging handle on the CAR-15, setting the safety on and swinging the collapsible stock Colt's muzzle away from the bike and into the empty street. "It's not a Neutron bomb," he said. "Look over there."

He watched over his shoulder as the girl turned, looking in the general direction the CAR-15 was pointed. Scrawny but healthy trees were growing in a small square. "No," he said. "Everybody just left—or mostly everybody."

He glanced down to his watch, then back up the street.

"Where's Paul?" Natalie asked. He could feel her breath against his right ear.

"That's just what I was starting to ask myself," Rourke muttered, his voice a whispered monotone. "It might not be a bad idea, you know, for you to reach around my waist, unbuckle my gunbelt and put that Python on yourself—you might need the spare ammo on the belt."

Rourke felt the woman's hands and arms encircling his waist.

He helped her undo the buckle, craned his neck and watched as she slung the cammie-patterned gunbelt from her right shoulder across to her left hip, the Python in its flap holster on her left side, butt forward.

"You ready?"

The girl took the massive revolver from the leather and nodded.

"Okay," Rourke said softly, starting the bike down the center of the deserted street.

He stared ahead of them, whispering over the hum of the Harley's engine, "Did you just see something moving in that space between buildings about twenty-five yards back?"

"On the right?"

"Yeah . . ."

"Man with a rifle, I thought, but wasn't sure."

"Yeah . . . okay . . . I'm going up to the end of the block here and turn down and back into that secondary street Paul was coming up. That's when we should hit it."

"Brigands?" the girl said softly, her voice even, calm.

"Maybe worse—people defending what's left of their town," Rourke answered, curving the bike wide to the right and then arcing left into the far lane of the intersecting street—also seemingly deserted. The secondary street was coming up on the left, and as Rourke's eyes scanned back and forth there was still no sign of Paul Rubenstein.

He pulled the Harley into another wide arc, cutting left into the secondary street. As he started the big machine along the uneven pavement, he heard Natalie behind him, whispering, her voice hoarse, "John—on your right!"

Rourke perfunctorily glanced to his right, raised his right hand in a small wave and whispered back to the girl. "Yeah . . . I saw them." As they cruised slowly down the street on each side of them now armed men and women were appearing, stepping out of doorways, from behind overturned cars and trucks, closing in like a wall behind them. "Relax," he rasped. "If they wanted to shoot first they'd be doing it by now."

"I don't take much comfort from that," the girl said, almost angrily.

Suddenly, the girl almost screamed, "Look—up ahead—they've got Paul!"

"Yeah . . . I see it," Rourke said softly. Rubenstein was on his knees at the end of the street, his hands tied out, arms stretched between the rear axle of an overturned truck and a support column for one of the smaller factory loading docks. There was a young man standing beside Rubenstein, an assault rifle with fixed bayonet in his hands, the point of the bayonet at the side of Rubenstein's throat. "I don't know who these people are—but they aren't brigands either. At least not the type we've seen."

"John—go back!" Rubenstein screamed, the man beside Rubenstein then pressing the bayonet harder against Rubenstein's throat, silencing him.

Rourke stopped the Harley he rode about twenty feet in front of Rubenstein, slowly but deliberately swinging the CAR-15 in the direction of the man with the bayonet, his right fist clenched on the rifle's pistol grip.

"Who are you people?" Rourke asked slowly, his eyes scanning the knot of young men and women, all of them armed. He had counted—including the ones walled behind him now and blocking his way out—perhaps twenty-five, more or less evenly divided male and female and all of them in their middle to late teens.

"We'll ask the questions," a dark-haired boy with what looked like acne on his left cheek shouted.

"Then ask away, boy," Rourke said, glaring at the young man but keeping the muzzle of his CAR-15 trained where it had been—on the one holding the bayonet to Rubenstein's throat.

"Who are you?" the acne-faced voice came back, unsteadily but loud.

Rourke exhaled hard, saying in a voice not much above a whisper, "John T. Rourke, the girl here says she's Natalie Timmons and the man your pal has on the ground there is Paul Rubenstein. Just wayfarin' strangers, kid."

"Who are you with?" the leader shouted.

"You don't listen too good, do you boy?" Rourke said, shooting an angry glance at the perhaps eighteen-year-old belonging to the voice.

"I mean what group are you with?"

"Well," Rourke began. "I belonged to a motor club before the war. That do you any good?"

"Cut out the smart-ass routine, mister!"

"Boy," Rourke said slowly, menacingly, "you talk that way to me once more and you've got an extra navel—just a shade over five and a half millimeters wide," and Rourke gestured with the CAR-15, then settled it back covering the man guarding Paul Rubenstein. "Now—what are you doing with my friend here?"

"You came to steal from us, didn't you?" the acne-faced leader shouted.

"What—you deaf kid," Rourke said. "Learn to control your voice. If you've got something I want, I'll deal with you for it. If there's something I want that nobody's got but it's there anyway, yeah, I'll take it. Promissory notes and money and checks and credit cards aren't much good these days, I understand."

"We call ourselves the Guardians."

"Well—how nice for you. What are you the "Guardians" of?"

As Rourke asked the question, he could hear Natalie trying to whisper to him. He leaned back away from his handlebars and caught her voice, "Rourke—behind us—six of them coming."

"We are the Guardians—"

"You ask me," Rourke said, "I think you're the crazies, myself." Suddenly Rourke's body tensed as he leaned forward. His tone softening, he addressed all the young men and women there, shouting, "How many of you have marks on your faces like he has—or elsewhere on your bodies?"

A girl stepped forward out of the knot around the leader. Rourke saw the acnelike marks on both her cheeks and neck. "Who are you?" she demanded.

The six advancing from behind Rourke were getting closer. He could see them now out of the corner of his left eye.

"Where were you the night of the war?" Rourke asked, slowly.

"Were we anywhere near a blast site, do you mean?" the girl asked, almost laughing, her dark eyes crinkling into a strange smile.

"We were," the acne-faced leader began. "And we know what we've got. But guarding here is what we do."

The girl beside the leader of the young people went on, "We were away on a senior class field trip. By the time the bus ran out of gas and we walked back here everyone had gone. We knew where there were some guns and we've been running the town ever since. We know we've all got radiation sickness, we're all dying. But we're guarding the town until our families get back. We're doing this for them."

Rourke eyed the six, now just a few feet behind himself and Natalie. "What if they don't come back?" Rourke asked slowly.

"We'll guard the town until the last of us has died," the girl beside the leader said flatly.

"Anybody with sores like that is going to die—and soon and painfully," Rourke told her.

"We know!" the girl beside the leader shouted back to him, her voice shrill.

"John!" Natalie rasped hard in Rourke's ear.

"I know," he muttered, catching sight of the six readying their weapons behind him. Then turning back to the leader, Rourke asked, "What do you want us for—let my friend go and we'll be on our way."

"People like you—violent people, people without a home or a town—you caused the war. You deserve to die!" the leader shouted.

"If you all feel that way, you're all crazy," Rourke said calmly. He was watching the leader now, but out of the corner of his eye saw the young man guarding Rubenstein take a half-step back, drawing the bayonet rifle rearward for a thrust. He heard Paul Rubenstein shouting, "John!"

"I am sorry," Rourke said so softly that he felt perhaps no one heard him, then pulled the trigger on the CAR-15, twice, cutting down the young man with the bayonet just as the thrust began for Paul Rubenstein's throat.

Rourke's left hand flashed across his body, snatching one of the stainless Detonics .45s, his thumb jacking back the hammer as the gun ripped from the Alessi shoulder holster, his left trigger finger working once, the slug catching the leader between the eyes and hurtling the already dying youth back against the knot of followers around him.

Rourke started to shout to Natalie, but as he turned, he could see her, already off the bike and in a crouch, the Python in both her fists, firing into the six attackers coming up behind him.

Rourke started the bike forward, the Detonics slipping into his trouser belt, replaced in his left hand by the black-chromed Sting IA, and as he reached Rubenstein he hacked out with the double-edge blade, cutting the ropes on Rubenstein's left wrist, then the right, tossing the younger man the once fired .45.

Rubenstein, still on his knees, looked up at Rourke, shouting, "They're only kids, John!"

Rourke, his eyes hard, bit his lower lip, then shouted, "God help me—I know that, damn it!"

Three of the heavily armed youths were rushing toward Rourke already and he swung the CAR-15 on line and opened up, cutting them down. He glanced back to Rubenstein, the younger man finishing a knee smash on a beefy-looking boy of about eighteen, beside Rubenstein's bike. Natalie was reloading the Python and as she brought it on line, with her left hand she brushed the hair back from her face. For an instant, Rourke wasn't in the middle of a life or death gun battle with a gang of bloodthirsty kids all dying of radiation poisoning—he was back in Latin America. The gun she held wasn't a Python—it was an SMG. And the hair was blonde, but the gesture, the stance, the set of the eyes—they hadn't been blue in those days—was exactly the same.

There was a burst of submachine gun fire from his right and Rourke turned, seeing Rubenstein firing the German MP-40—the "Schmeisser"—into the dirt at the feet of three attackers. The youths kept coming and—the reluctance was visible in the way Rubenstein moved—Rourke watched as the younger man raised the muzzle of the SMG and fired. Rourke turned back toward Natalie. He knew now that wasn't her name. His gun in her hands was silent. Rourke's eyes scanned the area around him, the muzzle of his CAR-15 sweeping the air. There were bodies, but no living combatants. He counted ten dead—meaning at least fifteen still out there somewhere.

In an instant, Rubenstein was standing beside him, the girl who called herself Natalie turning and facing him. The girl spoke first. "I was beginning to think you never were going to make your move—I know why you waited. I think I realized before you did that they were all dying of radiation sickness."

Rourke looked down to his bike, taking his .45 back from Rubenstein and swapping in a fresh load, saying to the girl, "I remembered where I saw you—South America, a few years ago. You were a blonde—I think your eyes were green. But it was you. Contact lenses?" He looked up at the girl then, taking off his sunglasses and pushing them back past his forehead into his hair.

He squinted past the midday sun at her.

"They were contact lenses," she nodded. "But what now?"

"You mean about this, or about my remembering you?" Rourke asked softly.

"Whatever," the girl said.

"Let's stick to this for now—we can worry about the other thing later. We still need supplies. Looks like the town was abandoned for some reason. Probably, if we look hard enough, we can find what we need. Still gotta worry about those kids sniping at us."

"I can't understand this!" Rubenstein almost cried.

"What?" Rourke asked.

"We just killed ten perfectly decent kids, or at least they were. What's happening?"

"Sometimes when people realize they're dying, it's almost as if they step out of themselves," Rourke began. "Those kids were smart enough to realize what was happening to them, and they focused their energies, their thoughts—everything—on guarding this town. Kind of calculated mass hysteria. It didn't matter to them that it was wholly irrational, impossible, even that they knew I was right that no one was coming back here for them. Probably once the first one started noticing what was happening and then some of the others started coming up with the symptoms they just made a sort of pact. Kids are big on that sort of thing—pacts, blood oaths."

Rubenstein stared into the dirt, saying, "That radiation poisoning thing—just because they were in the wrong spot at the wrong time. It could have been us, instead."

"It still could be us," Rourke said quietly, putting on his sunglasses again. "When was the last time you checked the Geiger counter?"

"Sometimes I like it better when you don't say anything—like you usually do," the girl, Natalie, said, holstering Rourke's revolver.

Chapter Twenty-Seven

Rourke sat by the small Coleman stove, water still steaming from the yellow kettle, the red-foil Mountain House package in his left hand, a table spoon he'd found held in his right. He gave the contents of the foil package a last stir and scooped a spoonful of the contents up and put it in his mouth, then leaned back against the rear bumper of the pickup truck. "I love their beef stroganoff," Rourke commented, almost to himself.

"This stuff is terrific!" Rubenstein said.

"What have you got there, Paul?" Rourke asked.

"Chicken and rice," Rubenstein answered, his speech garbled because his mouth was full.

"Next time try some of this—the noodles in it are great, too."

Natalie, still stirring at the contents of her packet, looked at Rourke across the glow of the small Coleman lamp between the three of them, saying, "Well—now that we've found food, plenty of water, gasoline and a four-wheel drive pickup—what next?"

Rourke leaned forward, looking at the full spoon inches from his mouth, saying, "Don't forget we found cigars for me and cigarettes for you."

"That guy really had the stuff put away under that warehouse," Rubenstein commented, his mouth still full.

"Yeah—too bad he never got a chance to use it, apparently," Rourke sighed, finally consuming the spoonful.

"I can't understand that town," the girl said. "Why hadn't the brigands been there?"

"Well . . ." Rourke began.

"And why and where did all the people who lived there go?" the girl went on.

Rourke looked at her, took another spoonful of the food and began again. "The way I've got it figured, everybody in the town just evacuated—I don't know to where. When those kids showed up and started shooting everything that moved, I guess the lead elements of the brigand force probably pulled in there, got killed and never reported back. There are two kinds of field commanders. Whoever's in charge of the brigands apparently isn't the kind of guy who took losing a squad of men as a personal challenge. He just went around the town, maybe figuring the people there were too well armed. That means he's smart. He's not out to conquer and hold territory—he's just out to keep his people going on whatever they can plunder. I'd figure right about now he's got a dicey job. Could be several hundred of them, no discipline, drinking up everything they can get their hands on and staying smashed most of the time on drugs. Be like tryin' to control a gang of alcoholic gorillas—or maybe more like the stereotype of Vikings. Come in and strike hard, earn a reputation for brutality, retreat or withdraw fast and steal everything that isn't nailed down."

"Then they're still ahead of us," the girl stated more than asked.

"Yeah—and strong and probably by now spoiling for a good fight. I wouldn't worry. We're bound to bump into them," Rourke concluded, finishing the last of his food packet and crumpling it in his hand, then tossing it in a sack in the back of the truck.

"Why did you go to all that trouble?" the girl asked, looking at him earnestly.

"What—not just throw it on the ground? Enough of the country's ruined; why ruin more of it?" Rourke reached into his shirt pocket and pulled out a cigar, lighting it with the Zippo.

"Here—give me that, the lighter," the girl said and Rourke snapped it closed and tossed it to her. She stared at it a moment—the initials "J.T.R." on it—turned it over in her hands and lit her cigarette, then snapped it closed, looked at it a moment and threw it back to him.

"Am I starting to ring bells for you, too—can you remember me yet?"

"I don't know what you mean," Natalie told him, smiling.

"Hey—" Rubenstein said, brightly. "Why don't we all have a drink? I mean, I could use one—we got six bottles back in the truck. "Where'd you put 'em, John?"

"In the front right-hand corner," Rourke answered, not looking at Rubenstein, but looking at the dark-haired, blue-eyed girl instead, her face glowing in the warm light of the lantern. "There, just in front of my bike—I wrapped 'em up in an old towel I found. Go get one if you want."

Rourke glanced away from the girl and toward the truck. They'd found the warehouse just as darkness had started, and Rubenstein—good at finding things, Rourke decided—had uncovered the doorway leading into the small basement under the main floor of the place. Using one of the flashlights they'd taken a long time back from the geological supply shop in Albuquerque, Rourke had gone down and discovered the cache of supplies. All the ammunition had been .308 and Rourke had left it, not having need of additional ammo for the Steyr. But the vast supplies of Mountain House freeze-dried foods, water and gasoline had been welcome. They had taken comparatively little, resealing the door after themselves just in case the original owner was still alive. They'd found the pickup truck a half-hour earlier and with the added supplies decided on taking it along—the keys had been in it.

The girl had been left on guard outside the warehouse while Rourke and Rubenstein had done the loading, the most awkward thing being getting the Harleys aboard the truck and securing them. There had been no further signs of the doomed, insane "Guardians" they had confronted earlier. As the three had started to leave—darkness already having fallen—the girl had said to Rourke, "You're a doctor—isn't there something you can do for them?"

"Mercy killing?" he'd asked quietly. "And beyond

that, they're beyond help. If I had a hospital, some specialists in nuclear medicine, we could make them comfortable, prolong their lives by a few weeks, maybe. But the result'd be the same. The longer we keep moving on the greater the chance we have of the same thing happening to us."

They'd driven in silence after that, Rubenstein starting to whistle occasionally, some lonely-sounding tune Rourke couldn't quite identify. The pickup's headlights didn't go on once, as Rourke headed slowly along the road and after several miles turned off into the desert, nothing more than moonlight lighting his way. He'd walked back along the route and carefully obliterated their tire treads from the sand then, and when Rubenstein—as usual—had asked why, Rourke had merely said, "I want to sleep with both eyes closed tonight—maybe."

Rubenstein passed the bottle around—Jack Daniels, square bottle, black label—and Rourke took a hard pull on it, leaning back again by the light blue pickup's rear bumper. He looked at the girl as she drank and when she handed the bottle back to Rubenstein, said, "Have you remembered me yet?"

She just shook her head, the same gesture of brushing her hair from her face, making Rourke see her again as she had been years earlier, as he remembered her. She took another drink, and so did Rubenstein.

Rourke alternately watched the stars overhead and stared at his watch, only once more taking a drink. As he watched the glowing tip of his second cigar, already burnt to nearly a stump in his fingers, he turned, startled. Rubenstein was snoring, the bottle beside him more than half-empty. A smile crossed Rourke's lips.

"I must trust you," the girl started to say, standing up, weaving a bit as she walked around the lantern, then sitting down on the ground beside him.

"Why do you say that?" Rourke said as she picked up Rubenstein's bottle and drank from it. She offered it to Rourke and he wiped his sleeve across it and took a tiny swallow, then returned it to her.

"I trust—trust you, because otherwise I wouldn't let myself get drunk around you! You will have to promise me," she whispered, leaning toward him, smiling, "that if I start to talk, you won't listen—I mean if I say anything personal or like that."

She leaned toward him and he turned to face her and she kissed him on the mouth. "There, Mister Goodie-goodie," she laughed. "That didn't hurt, did it?"

Rourke looked into her eyes, watched her eyes, the sad and beautiful set they had, the deepness of their blue. He whispered, "No—it didn't hurt. The problem is it felt too good." He dropped the cigar butt on the ground and kicked it out with the heel of his boot, folding the girl into his left arm and letting her head sink against his chest. In a moment he could hear her breathing, slow and even against him. He looked up at the stars, the warmth of the woman in his arms only heightening the loneliness. He wondered what was in the stars—was there another world where men and women hadn't been foolish enough to destroy everything as it was now destroyed here. As the girl stirred against him, Rourke closed his eyes. Her breathing, its evenness, and the warmth of her body in the desert cold . . . he opened his eyes, breathing hard and stared down at her in the light of the lamp. He eased her head down onto the rolled-up blanket beside him and stood up to put out the lantern. He stared back at her profile in the semi-darkness, his fists bunching hard together. He was a man who had always screamed inwardly, silently, and this time he screamed the name "Sarah!"

Chapter Twenty-Eight

Sarah Rourke climbed stiffly into the saddle, her stomach still cramping when she moved too quickly or bent, but the cramps lessening in intensity. The previous night's dinner had stayed with her although she hadn't eaten much, and at breakfast that morning there had been none of the accustomed nausea. After she had awakened that first morning, with Michael's help they had found a better, more permanent campsite as close as possible to the site they had used the night of her collapse. She had barely been able to mount up then, but with Michael leading her horse, they somehow had managed.

As she straightened in the saddle now, she thought of Michael and the last few days since she had drunk the contaminated water and been rendered virtually helpless. The boy was a constant source of amazement to her. Lying virtually helpless on her back at that time, the stomach cramps, the nausea—Michael had been her hands, her feet, keeping the girls and himself fed, feeding and watering the horses. Once, there had been noises, voices from far along on the other side of the forested area from where they were, and the boy had brought her the .45 automatic pistol, then gathered the girls next to him and waited silently beside her until the voices had died away, the noise ceased. She turned now in the saddle, still awkwardly because of her stiffness, and looked at the boy.

"You're the finest son anyone could want, Michael," she said to him, her voice still not sounding quite right to her.

"Why did you say that, Mom?" the boy said, smiling at her, his brown hair falling across his forehead.

"I just wanted to," she said. She moved her knees too fast and the cramps started to return, but she straightened up in the saddle as Tildie started forward along the trail into Tennessee.

Chapter Twenty-Nine

Rourke brought the Harley to a fast stop, skidding his feet into the dirt and squinting against the morning sunlight despite the dark aviator-style sunglasses he wore. His face and his body under his clothes were bathed in sweat. He shifted the CAR-15's web sling off his shoulder, the outline of the sling visible in dark wet stains on his shirt. He had cut across country, backtracking for a while until he had come across the lead elements of the paramilitary force. With his liberated field glasses he had spotted the familiar face of the officer he and Rubenstein had encountered days earlier by the abandoned truck trailer when they had been resupplying with ammunition. The force consisted of what Rourke estimated as close to three hundred and fifty men, traveling in trucks and jeeps in a ragged wedge formation along the road, outriders on dirt bikes paralleling their movements and working back and forth, up and down the convoy line like herders moving cattle or sheep. He timed them and judged they were making approximately fifty miles per hour, and with their numbers there was no reason to suppose they wouldn't press on for fourteen or more hours per day—as long as daylight lasted.

Rourke had cut ahead then, the convoy several hours behind where he had left Paul Rubenstein and the girl who called herself Natalie. And now, as he watched the road below him, the tight bend the highway followed, he could see the brigands. There were more than two dozen long-haul eighteen-wheeler trucks at their center, traveling four abreast, consuming the entire highway space, squads of motorcycle riders in front and in back and on the shoulders, all heavily armed. Though he had no way of telling what or who might be inside the trucks, he judged the strength of the brigand force at better than four hundred men and women. For some reason he couldn't fathom, they were heading back in the direction of Van Horn, speed approximately fifty miles per hour. A smile crossed Rourke's lips, but then vanished quickly. As he watched the brigand column began turning off the road, moving into a long, single column and heading into the desert.

"Shit!" he muttered, dropping the field glasses and staring down into his hands. The change of direction into the desert would keep the brigands ahead of him, and the paramilitary force was still behind him. Rourke reslung the CAR-15 on his right shoulder and revved up his bike. The brigands' turning had forced his hand, he realized, and any way he decided to go, the odds for staying alive were dropping.

Chapter Thirty

Rourke had left early in the morning, awakening the slightly hung-over Rubenstein to let him know his intentions, letting the girl continue to sleep. As Rourke slowed the Harley and drove it up the grade into the sheltered campsite where the truck was parked, he spotted Rubenstein sitting by the Coleman stove, a cup of coffee in both hands, his glasses off. Natalie was standing by the front of the truck and all Rourke could see of her as he eased the bike to a halt was her back.

"I didn't recognize you without your glasses," Rourke said to Rubenstein, smiling.

"Shut off the motor, huh? My head is—"

Rourke laughed, killing the Harley's engine and dismounting, then walking over toward Rubenstein. Rourke set the CAR-15 against the bumper of the truck and dropped to a crouch beside the younger man, snatching a cup and pouring himself some coffee. "What's with her?"

"What? Oh—I don't know—she's been that way

ever since she woke up and found you were gone," Rubenstein answered, his voice shaky.

"So what did you find out, Rourke?"

Rourke looked up. It was the girl, hands on her hips, feet a little apart, tiny chin jutted forward, her eyes fixed and staring at him. "You look cheerful this morning," Rourke told her, then, "What I found out was that the paramilitary is a few hours behind us with a large force. The brigands are a few hours ahead of us with a large force. Even larger than the paramils. If we bump into the paramils, we've had it. Paul and I had a run-in with one of their patrols before we bumped into you. The officer who commanded the patrol is with the paramil force I saw. He'll spot us, we'll get shot—and probably you too since you're with us. They're southwest of us now, heading northeast along the road. The brigands were heading southwest, and for a while I thought they'd run into the paramils, but then they turned off into the desert. Probably going to be staying in this area for a while."

"So what do we do?" the girl asked him.

"Can't go southwest and run into the paramils. Just have to take our chances on butting up against the brigands."

Rubenstein, rubbing his eyes with his hands, said, "But if we do run into the brigands, what then?"

"Well," Rourke said slowly, staring into his coffee, "we sort of promised that woman with the refugees that we'd look for that blonde guy who killed her baby. I guess we can do that, then move on."

"How many brigands are there?" Natalie asked, her voice tense.

"Better than four hundred, I make it. But we can't just stay here—the paramils will find us. I make it that within the next few days both units should lock horns—looks unavoidable with their sizes—couldn't miss one another. Then maybe we can get clear of the area."

"But what do we do until that happens?" Rubenstein asked.

"Stay just shy of the brigands and try to pass around them—if we can. If we can't, though, we only have one additional option. We join 'em."

"What!" Rubenstein exclaimed.

Rourke lit a cigar and leaned back against the truck. "They've never seen us, must have picked up a lot of their force from bikers driftin' in two or three at a time. If we have to, we'll fake it."

"And what if they don't buy that?" the girl asked, her voice emotionless.

"Then we'll buy it," Rourke answered slowly, then sipped at his coffee.

Chapter Thirty-One

Samuel Chambers, necktie at half-mast, suitcoat gone, two empty packs of Pall Malls crumpled on the small table beside his chair, the standing glass ashtray overflowing with cigarette butts, squinted against the yellow lamplight from the desk. He glanced at his watch. The conference had gone on longer than he had expected without breaking. The thought came to him that if this was what being the president of the United States was really like, he could see why the job had aged all the men who had gone before him. "Heavy lies the head," he muttered to himself, lighting another cigarette and wishing he hadn't from the bad taste in his mouth.

He looked at the notes he'd taken on the yellow legal pad on his lap, pondering silently if it would work, if the country could be sewn back together even temporarily. Parts of Louisiana and all of Texas had been consolidated into one martial law district, the paramilitary commander, Soames—Chambers didn't like the man and trusted him less—taking charge of internal matters because of the sheer numbers of his force and the capability to recruit more. The air force colonel, Darlington, would use his troops and the navy forces to handle border defense, using the stores of National Guard supplies to help with this. The National Guard unit—small—would function as a traditional army unit, but outside the borders of this "kernel" of a nation. They would execute clandestine military operations against the Soviet invaders as required, but, more important, try to establish communications links with civil and military authorities in other parts of the country.

Chambers smiled bitterly—he was too much of a realist to assume there were not other men now calling themselves president of the United States, or at the least taking on the concurrent authority the title implied. He tried telling himself, convincing himself, that it would work. "I don't believe it," he muttered, then lit another cigarette.

When dawn came, he would be taking a military flight into Galveston to personally assess rumors of a Soviet presence there, as well as to wrap up his personal affairs. All his advisors had warned against the flight. Perhaps, he reflected, that was the first time he had actually felt like a president. He had listened carefully, asked questions, explained his reasoning and then—in the face of the irrefutable logic of his "advisors"—flatly stated he didn't "give a damn." He wanted to see Galveston one more time.

Chapter Thirty-Two

Rourke hadn't caught the name of the town as he, Natalie and Rubenstein had passed it. There was smoke trailing in a wide black line across the sky from where the town should have been, and Rourke thought silently that likely the town was no longer there. There was gunfire discernible in the distance and faint, almost ghostly sounds, Rourke mentally labeled them, that could either have been the wind or human screams. The brigands had turned back out of the desert early that morning, placing Rourke, Rubenstein and the girl sandwiched between the brigands and the paramils, now perhaps a day's march or less apart. Rourke braked the light blue pickup truck on the top of a rise, out of years of driving habit pulling onto the shoulder and out of the main northeastern-bound lanes, despite the fact that there was no traffic.

Rourke cut the engine and stepped out, stretching after the long ride, watching the dark clouds moving in from the northwest. Already the breeze, which had been hot that morning, was turning cool, and he shivered slightly as he walked to the edge of the road shoulder and stared over the guard rail toward the remains of the town. Below the level of the smoke, there were large dust clouds from vehicles—many of them, Rourke reflected.

"Are they down there?"

Rourke turned around, bracing his right hand against the butt of the Python on his right hip, looking at Natalie. "Yeah—they're down there, all right. And I make it the paramils aren't far behind us—I think it's now or never."

"How about never?" Rubenstein said through the open passenger side window, forcing a smile.

"He's right—Rourke is," Natalie volunteered. "We're better off with the brigands than caught between them and the paramils."

"Let's go down then and introduce ourselves," Rourke said softly, starting back around the front of the pickup and climbing into the driver's seat. He gunned the engine to life, out of years of habit looked over his left shoulder to see if there was traffic—there wouldn't be, he realized rationally—and edged out onto the highway.

Rourke reached down to his waist and tried unbuckling the gunbelt, then turned and looked at the girl, feeling her right hand crossing his abdomen and seeing her turn awkwardly in the seat between himself and Rubenstein. She undid the buckle and he leaned forward in the seat and she slipped the belt from around his waist. "You want me armed again?" she asked.

"Yeah—might be advisable," Rourke answered.

"You seemed to do pretty well with that Python the last time—no sense messing with success."

The girl rebuckled the Ranger Leather Belt and slung it diagonally across her body, the holster with the six-inch Metalifed .357 Magnum revolver hanging on her left side by her hip bone, the dump pouches with the spare ammo crossing her chest between her breasts. Rourke looked back to the road, hearing the sounds of Rubenstein checking the German MP-40, the gun the younger man still called a "Schmeisser."

Rourke shifted his shoulders under the weight of the twin Detonics stainless .45s in the double Alessi shoulder rig, then reached into his breast pocket and snatched a cigar. He fished the lighter from his Levis and as he did, the girl took it from his hand and worked it for him, holding the blue yellow-flamed Zippo just right, below the tip of the cigar so the flame could be drawn up into it. "Where'd you learn to light a cigar?" he asked, nodding his thanks.

"My father smoked them," the girl said, then closed the lighter and handed it back to him.

"What else did your father do?" Rourke asked, clamping the cigar in the left side of his mouth between his teeth and turning the steering wheel into an easy right onto an off ramp from the highway.

"He was a doctor—a medical doctor," the girl answered, "like you are. When I was a little girl," she said, "I was always going to grow up and be his nurse. But he died when I was eighteen," she added, her voice sounding strange and without the easy confidence he had become accustomed to hearing in it.

"I'm sorry," Rourke said quietly.

"I guess time makes everyone an orphan, doesn't it," Rubenstein said, sounding as though he were speaking more to himself than to Rourke or the girl. Rourke turned and looked at Rubenstein, saying nothing.

"Over there!" the girl said suddenly.

Rourke glanced back down the road and to his left. In the distance—in what must have been an athletic field—he could see a crude circle of semitrailer trucks and several dozen motorcycles, all moving slowly, dust filling the air around them. There were gunshots now, over the noise of the truck and bike engines, and again Rourke thought he heard what could have been screams, coming from inside the circle of trucks.

"What the hell are they doing?" Rubenstein asked.

"I think I know," the girl answered.

"They've apparently gotten their mass executions into some kind of ritual, working themselves up into a frenzy before they do them, terrifying the victims too." As Rourke spoke, the trucks began slowing down, the dust thinning. "And it looks like they're ready for their number," he added.

"I didn't think there were so many crazy people in the world," Rubenstein remarked, his eyes wide and staring at the trucks and the gradually diminishing dust cloud.

"Some people, maybe most people," Natalie began, "can't handle violence emotionally—they sort of revert to savages and along with that goes all the rest of it—"

Rourke finished for her, turning their truck off the

road and crossing onto the far edge of the football field. "It's the reptilian portion of the brain coming to the fore. A lot of work was done on it just before the war. The reptile portion of the brain is the part obsessed with ritual and violence, and sometimes there's little to differentiate between the two. You look at just normal things—fraternity initiations, street gangs, all sorts of things like that. The violence and the ritual eventually so intermingle that you can't have one without the other; one causes the other."

"Like rape, Paul," Natalie said. "Or sex-related murders. Is intercourse or death the purpose of the act, or just something that happens as a result, the act itself being the purpose?"

"I think Behavioral Psych 101 just let out, gang," Rourke said softly, starting to slow the pickup truck as he wove it between two of the nearest semis and into the circle.

The girl beside him unsnapped the thumbreak opening flap on the holster with the big Python. Rubenstein pulled back the bolt on the "Schmeisser."

"Be cool," Rourke cautioned, stopping the pickup truck in the approximate center of the circle. In front of the hood were perhaps fifty people, mostly women and children, a few older men, some of them still in pajamas or nightgowns, their clothes torn, their faces dirty and their eyes filled with terror. Rourke whispered, "This must be the place," and shut off the key on the pickup truck and swung open the driver's side door and stepped out, the CAR-15 slung under his right shoulder now, his fist wrapped around the pistol grip.

The knot of townspeople stared at him, almost as though they collectively made one frightened organism. He looked away from them, rolling the cigar in the corner of his mouth, his chin jutting forward, his legs slightly apart. He turned and looked behind the pickup truck. Already perhaps a dozen or more of the motorcyclists from the brigand gang were walking toward him, some of the drivers of the eighteen-wheelers were climbing down from their cabs and walking toward him as well. Rourke squinted against the sun and shot a glance skyward—the entire northwestern quadrant was so gray it almost seemed black by contrast to the deep blue of the sky above him. The wind was picking up, making tiny dust devils around his feet.

"Who the fuck are you?" The voice came from a tall man, Rourke's height or better, but an easy fifty pounds heavier, wearing a dark blue denim shirt with the sleeves cut off, leaving frayed edges across his rippling shoulder muscles. He wore a military-style shoulder holster, a stag-gripped .45 automatic riding in it on the left side of his chest. In his right hand was a riot shotgun, with extension magazine and a sling, web materialed, blowing now slightly in the wind like the man's dark, greasy-looking hair.

"Rourke—he's Paul Rubenstein, the girl's name is Natalie." Out of the corner of his left eye, Rourke could see Rubenstein, standing half-inside the cab of the pickup truck, the MP-40 submachine gun held lazily in his left hand across the roof of the cab. The girl was already out of the pickup truck, standing beside Rourke and a little behind him.

"The goddamn names don't mean shit to me,

man—what d'ya want here?"

Rourke sighed, a small cloud of the gray cigar smoke filtering through his nostrils as he rolled the cigar in the corner of his mouth. "Got the paramils after us—we hit a truck back a ways and boosted some ammo and stuff. Killed a coupla their guys gettin' away—figured you might be able to use a few extra people who could handle a gun. You got those suckers less than a day behind you and you guys leave plenty of tracks," and Rourke gestured over his right shoulder with the cigar toward the townspeople huddled behind him.

"We got enough people can handle a gun, buddy—what the hell we need you for?"

"You're amateurs, I'm professional—I'm worth at least any three of your guys."

"Bullshit," the big guy laughed. "I'm gonna kill me these little pieces of scared dogshit behind you, then we'll see just how good you are."

The big man started forward and Rourke, the cigar back in his mouth, took a step to his right, blocking the big man's path. "You know," Rourke whispered, his face inches from the face of the brigand, "you guys are real assholes."

The brigand turned, his face red with rage, his hands starting to move. Rourke—again whispering—said, "Go ahead—from here I can't miss," and he edged the CAR-15 slightly forward, the muzzle almost touching the bigger man's stomach just above the belt buckle. "See, you guys keep knockin' off the civilian population, after a while, no matter how many of 'em you kill, they're gonna finally get just mad enough to band together and come after you guys—then you'll have them *and* the paramils on your neck. Same thing happened to the Romans, two thousand years later it happened to the Nazis when they marched into the Ukraine in Russia. How would you like snipers behind every rock, explosives under every bridge? It can happen to you, friend."

"What d'ya want? I'm askin' again."

"I told you—me and my friends wanna join up for the duration," Rourke told him.

"You're as good as any three of us, huh?" the bigger man said, a smile crossing his lips.

Rourke smiled back, nodding, the cigar now just a stump in the left corner of his mouth. "Easy." Rourke glanced toward the growing knot of brigands and their women collecting perhaps a yard behind the pickup's tailgate. He could see the warning look in Natalie's eyes, the worry written across Paul Rubenstein's sweat-dripping face.

Then, in a loud voice, the man shouted, "This man is named Rourke—he claims he's some kinda lousy professional—as good as any three of us. I need two men to help me show him different!" More than a dozen men, as big at least as the brigand standing inches away from Rourke, stepped out of the knot of onlookers. "You, ahh, you wanna pick 'em?" the brigand said, smiling.

"You the head honcho around here?" Rourke asked.

"Yeah—I'm the leader—you backin' out?"

"No, no—nothin' like that," Rourke said softly. "I was just wonderin' if you had your replacement picked yet."

"Bite my—"

"Not in front of the lady," Rourke said, gesturing with the CAR-15.

Loud again, so all the brigands could hear, apparently, the brigand leader shouted, "If Rourke wins, he and his people can join us and we let all them over there go and everythin'," and the brigand leader pointed toward the townspeople, visibly cringing now, some of the children crying out loud. "But if he don't," the brigand shouted then, "we kill him and the other guy and the little piece they got with 'em—after we all have some fun with her first, huh?" There was some laughter by the men who'd stepped forward for the contest, and from the crowd behind them as well.

"You pickin' them or me?" Rourke said.

"Hey—I'll pick," the brigand leader laughed, gesturing broadly with his outstretched hands.

Moisture was already falling on Rourke's hands and face, thunder rumbling in the sky off to his left, what sunlight there had been fading and replaced by a greenish glow that seemed to be in the air, something he felt he could almost reach out and touch. "Be quick about it, huh," Rourke said. "I don't feel like standin' around in the rain all day waitin' for you—guns, knives, what?"

The brigand leader looked at Rourke, his eyes traveling up and down, then said, "We fight bare-handed—Taco, Kleiger—up here—everybody back off and give us some room!"

"What's your name—don't like fightin' somebody if I don't know his name."

"Mike."

"I've got a son named Michael—he's tougher than you, though," Rourke smiled.

The brigand leader backed away, slipping the shoulder rig off his chest and wrapping the strap around it, then handing the holstered .45 and the riot shotgun into the crowd.

Rourke flipped the safety on the CAR-15 rasped, "Natalie!" and tossed the gun across the six feet or so separating them. The girl caught it in both hands, moving the sling onto her right shoulder and then diagonally across her body, the pistol grip settling in her comparatively tiny right fist. Rourke could hear the safety clicking off. He slipped off the shoulder rig, and both guns together, he handed it across the roof of the pickup cab to Rubenstein. "If I die, I'll will 'em to you," Rourke whispered to Rubenstein.

Already, the brigand leader—Mike—was stripping the denim shirt from his body, the muscles on his arms and chest and neck wet with sweat, rippling even in the greenish light that now seemed heavy on the air itself. Thunder was rumbling low, and the rain was now starting to dot the dust of the burnt-dry football field with dark spots, the smell of the air somehow fresher and cooler.

Rourke stripped off his own light blue shirt, palming the Sting IA and dropping it in his jeans pocket. The girl reached out her left hand and took the shirt.

Rourke walked forward, away from the truck, joining the three brigands already waiting for him, his moving close to them completing a ragged circle.

The brigand leader, his eyes bright and laughing,

shouted, "Kleiger here, he used to be an instructor in unarmed combat in the Marine Corps a few years back. Now Taco is kind of special—made his living ever since he was a kid as a bar fighter down in Mexico. See all them scars? Me, I did time once for killing a man once with my hands—I just crushed his skull with 'em."

"Well," Rourke said softly, "then I'll try and make you fellas look good so you don't get too embarrassed by all of this."

"Get him!" Mike roared, and the wiry guy called Taco, and then Kleiger—bigger than the brigand leader—started forward, slow, unhurried, relaxed looking. Rourke waited. Kleiger started feigning a low savate kick, then wheeled, his left fist flashing outward, but already Rourke had sidestepped, wheeling, his left foot cutting in low, catching Kleiger on the right side and knocking him off balance. Rourke sidestepped again, a solid right coming at him from the one called Taco. The blow glanced off the side of Rourke's head, stunning him, driving him back. As Taco followed with a left hook, Rourke blocked it with his right, smashing his own left in a short-arm blow to the solar plexus, then crossing his right into the left side of Taco's nose, following with his left foot into Taco's crotch, the foot arched and hammering in with the force of a brick through a mirror. Out of the corner of his eye, Rourke could see Kleiger, back on balance and roaring toward him. Rourke wheeled, feigning another low kick, then sidestepped fast to his left, lashing out with his right then his left hand, hammering into Kleiger's face and neck. As Kleiger stumbled back, the brigand leader, Mike, dove toward Rourke, knocking Rourke back and off his feet, the man's huge hands going for Rourke's neck, his right knee smashing upward, hammering against Rourke's right thigh, going for Rourke's crotch. Rourke hooked his right thumb in the left corner of Mike's mouth and ripped. As Mike's head started pulling away, Rourke freed his left fist and crossed Mike's jaw with a short jab, rolled away and hauled himself to his feet, punching a short knee raise upward into the doubled-over Mike's jaw, then smashing the toe of his right combat boot forward, into the brigand leader's teeth. Rourke's right hand held the man by the hair.

Kleiger was starting for Rourke again, and Rourke stepped back. Taco was up, his nose a mass of blood streaming down over his mouth and onto his naked, sweating chest. Both men edged slowly toward Rourke, Kleiger making his move then and starting a wheeling series of punches and kicks. Rourke backed off from the first series, then stepped forward, blocking a side-hammer blow from Kleiger's left, then smashing his own left down into the exposed left kidney, then jamming his left foot upward into Kleiger's crotch, his left hand in a straight-edge classic karate chop slashing across the left side of Kleiger's neck and knocking him away, Kleiger collapsing forward to the ground on his face.

But Taco was already coming at Rourke, his left fist flying outward and Rourke got a half-step back before Taco's fist impacted against his jaw. Rourke's head snapped back, Taco's right crossing up toward his face, and Rourke dodged it, almost whispering so Taco alone could hear him, "You know how some guys—" Rourke panted, "how some guys have a glass jaw—me, I'm just the opposite." Taco's left flashed forward again and Rourke let it come, dodging his head right just before impact, feeling the rush of air as the bloodied knuckles passed his face, then straight-arming Taco with his own left fist, then crossing with his right, then his left, then his right, hammering the brigand back, forcing him to his knees, then feigning a low right, but instead, hammering up with his right knee, catching Taco on the tip of the chin and snapping the head and neck back with an audible crack.

Rourke stepped away as Mike climbed to his feet, his lower lip split wide, blood and teeth spitting from his mouth as he tried to stand. Rourke lashed out with his left foot, catching Mike square in the face over the nose and driving him back to the ground.

Rourke wheeled, feeling, sensing rather than seeing or hearing, Kleiger coming for him. It was too late to step away, and as Kleiger's right foot punched toward Rourke's crotch, Rourke blocked the blow with both hands crossed in front of him, the scissor formed by his wrists and forearms taking its force. Kleiger's right heel of the hand was driving up for Rourke's nose, and Rourke wheeled, his left elbow coming up and knocking the blow aside, then his left hand snapping back and downward into the side of Kleiger's neck, Rourke's right already drawn back and driving forward, the middle knuckles of the hand bunched together and hammering into the base of Kleiger's nose, and rather than driving the bone upward into the brain, withdrawing, snapping back, leaving Kleiger stunned, reeling, no guard to block the series of short left jabs Rourke hammered now toward Kleiger's jaw. As Kleiger stumbled, Rourke crossed Kleiger's jaw with a go-for-broke right and the man fell, straight back, stiff, his head snapping hard against the dirt of the field, bouncing a little.

Rourke stood, waiting. Mike was moving on the ground. but not getting up. Taco was down for the count, Rourke felt, as was Kleiger.

"Natalie," Rourke shouted, perhaps a half-dozen feet from her, extending his left hand, watching as the CAR-15's sling slipped from her shoulder and the gun sailed from her right hand and toward him. He caught the rifle, shifting it into his right hand as he worked the safety off, his right fist wrapped around the pistol grip, as a dozen or so of the brigands started toward him in a rush. But Rourke heard a grunting sound, almost not human. Mike, the brigand leader, was on his knees, gesturing rapidly with his right hand, starting to talk, still spitting teeth and blood into the dirt, as the rain fell now in a thin mist, the clouds above them now darkening like the clouds in the northwest had been. The rain felt good against Rourke's body, the dirt and sweat intermingled there with spattered blood from the men he'd fought down.

"Wait!" Mike finally shouted. "He won—it was fair. Could've killed Kleiger—I saw—"

Mike gestured to some of the brigand men and women standing near him and a group of them hauled him to his feet and Rourke lowered the muzzle of the CAR-15 as they approached.

"I been thinkin'," Mike said, his speech hard to understand, the smashed teeth and the cracked lips having resulted in a lisplike effect. He was less than two yards from Rourke now. He started to speak again. "I been thinkin'—maybe you don't like to kill. So I got one more test—some stakes. You make it this time, you're in—but I don't think you're gonna make it."

Rourke looked at Mike, his voice low, saying, "You better hope I do—I'm a doctor and if somebody doesn't put some stitches into that lower lip of yours, you're gonna bleed to death."

Mike's eyes flickered, but he said nothing, then, "I want you to brace Deke—with guns."

"Who's Deke?" the girl said, before Rourke could answer.

Mike's eyes smiled a moment, then the brigand leader said, "He's my right-hand man—and he's so good with a piece you wouldn't believe your eyes, lady."

"Where is he?" Rourke asked.

"Right here," the voice answered and Rourke slowly turned to his right. There was a slim, blonde-haired man with a little imperial on his chin and pansy-blue eyes standing at the edge of the circle of brigands. Rourke's mind flashed back to the description the refugee woman had given of the man who'd shot her baby. This was the man. And on his right hip in a cut-away Hollywood-style fast-draw rig was a glinting, nickel-plated single-action revolver, the hammer spur built up, the butt canted rearward, muzzle forward. A heavy leather glove covered the man's left hand. Rourke knew the drill—he'd tried competitive fast-draw, had had good friends who competed in the sport. And he knew the light-speed draws a trained fast-draw man could make. "You want it now, or you wanna clean up so you make a good-lookin' corpse?" Deke said, an Aussie-style camouflage cowboy hat low over his eyes.

"Catch you in five," Rourke said and turned away.

Chapter Thirty-Three

Rourke stood by the cab of the pickup truck, Rubenstein trying to look casual with the MP-40 subgun in his hands, the bolt still locked open, just waiting for a touch of the trigger. As Rourke splashed canteen water on his face, he could feel Natalie's hands on his back, a handkerchief or something in her one hand and cool water being rubbed across him. He splashed water on his chest as well, then took his shirt and started to dry himself with it. He started to pull the shirt on, but heard the girl murmur, "Wait, John," and in a moment she was back with a fresh shirt for him from his pack.

As Rourke buttoned the shirt, stuffing the shirt-tails into his jeans, the girl came up beside him, the wet handkerchief in her hand, daubing at the right side of his mouth where he'd been cut. "I'm fine," Rourke whispered.

The girl—Natalie—stepped back. "You're not really going to do this—I mean you're good with guns and all, but this is like apples and oranges."

"She's right, John," Rubenstein commented, not looking at Rourke but watching the brigands. They had gone back to the trucks again, like natives in a death ritual, starting to drive them once more in a huge circle. But this time there was little dust; the rain was starting to fall more heavily now.

Rourke said, "You mean can I outdraw Deke? I don't think so, but there's a difference between drawing down on a timer and drawing down on a man—we'll see what happens."

"I've seen that kind of shooting before," the girl said.

"So have I," Rourke said softly, looking into her blue eyes. "He holds his hand on the gun butt, his left hand edged in front of the holster, and on the signal he rocks the gun out of the leather, the hand with the glove slaps the hammer back, fans it and the gun goes off. I couldn't see whether he's got the trigger tied back or not so he doesn't even have to bother touching it."

"He probably does," the girl said. "You want this?" she asked, gesturing toward the Python still slung diagonally across her body.

"No—I'll use these," he said, reaching into the cab of the truck and taking the Alessi double shoulder rig and the Detonics .45s. He put his arms into the shoulder harness and raised the harness up over his head and let it drop to his shoulders, then settled the holsters comfortably in place. He snatched the gun from the holster under his left armpit and buttoned out the magazine, then jacked back the slide, catching the chambered round. He reinserted the sixth round in the magazine and then slapped the spine of the magazine into his left palm, to seat the cartridges all the way back. He worked the stainless Detonics' slide several times, then locked the slide back, reinserted the magazine and let the slide stop down. The slide hammered forward. He raised the thumb safety, leaving the pistol cocked and locked, then settled it back into the holster, closing the snaps for the trigger guard speed break.

As he began the same ritual on the gun under his right arm, the girl looked up at him, her eyes hard, her jaw set. "You're crazy—you can't match that kind of speed with a conventional gun."

"These aren't conventional guns," Rourke told her. "Faster lock time than a standard .45, less felt recoil, good trigger pulls—the whole bit. Grip safeties are deactivated."

He left the second gun cocked and locked and replaced it in the holster under his right arm. "That doesn't have an ambidextrous safety," the girl said, insistent. "How will it do you any good to have a cocked and locked gun in your left hand?"

"Well," and Rourke withdrew the gun again. "Advantage of big hands." He craned his left thumb behind the backstrap of the pistol in his left hand and whiped off the safety, adding, "If I have to use it, I can this way. Probably one will be enough."

"You are crazy—you're going to get us all killed, all of them killed!" the girl said, her voice uncharacteristically shrill.

"You know," Rourke almost whispered to her, "you're a funny girl—you use a gun better than most men, you're pro all the way—know your stuff. Like I said, I remember you. Different hair, contacts for different eye color. I know who you are, why you were out there in the desert, and I know you and I are going to bump heads sooner or later. And you know it too. But you seem to genuinely care about those people over there, like you did with the refugees back down the road. And even though I know you know we're on opposite sides really, I honestly think you care what happens to me. Maybe I got problems going out there and facing Deke," Rourke said, gesturing toward the center of the circle of trucks, the trucks slowing now as the time approached for the gunfight, "but I think you've got problems in there," and Rourke gently tapped his right index finger against her left breast where her heart would be. "And you know just what I mean, lady."

She took a half-step back from him and said, "Remember that dumb line from all the old western movies? A man's gotta do what a man's gotta do? Well, that goes for women, too."

"I don't want us to wind up doin' a number with guns—you know."

The girl bit her lower lip, her voice barely audible, saying, "I didn't mean what I said the other night when I was drunk—about Mr. Goody-goody. Well, I meant it, but—"

Rourke sighed hard, then reached out and touched her face gently with his left hand. "You were right, anyway," he said and bent over and kissed her cheek.

The trucks had completely stopped now and as Rourke walked away from Rubenstein and Natalie, he thought how insane the whole thing was—the last quarter of the twentieth century and yet he was facing off in a nineteenth-century gunfight, with a gang of ritualistic murderers and renegades as the spectators, in a world that—for all Rourke knew—could itself have been in the last throes of death.

He could see Deke emerging from the crowd of brigands, the crowd itself splitting into two flanks with a clear space behind Rourke and space clearing behind Deke as well. The blonde-haired man—the baby-killer, Rourke reminded himself—had the Aussie hat dangling down his back now from a cord around his neck. The rain was falling more heavily, and already Rourke's fresh shirt was soaked through. The blonde man's hair hung in limp curls plastered against his forehead, the pansy-blue eyes riveted on Rourke as the two men moved slowly into position. From the corner of his right eye, Rourke could see Natalie, standing close beside Rubenstein, their eyes staring toward him. Rourke shot a glance toward Deke's right hip, then let his eyes drift upward to Deke's eyes. The two men were perhaps seven yards apart, Rourke gauged; it was the classic shootout distance—neither man could likely miss on the first shot. The single action Deke had strapped to his thigh with a heavy leather band at the base of the holster would be a .45 Long Colt calibre, the bullets themselves weightier than even a hardball .45 ACP load, the round an inherent man-stopper like the .45 ACP was.

The rain was heavy now, falling in sheets, blowing across the muddy surface of the field. Rourke's hair and face were wet, and he blinked the rain away from his eyelashes, knowing what would happen.

Deke's pansy-blue eyes set hard; the left hand with

the glove for fanning was twitching. Rourke dove right, into the mud, his right hand streaking toward the Detonics .45 under his left armpit, his first wrapping around the checkered rubber Pachmayr grips, the stainless pistol ripping from the leather. Deke's sixgun was out, his left hand streaking back faster than Rourke could see clearly, the big revolver belching fire and roaring like a grenade going off near his ears. Rourke hit the mud and rolled, the Detonics in his right hand firing once, then once again, the first round thudding into Deke's midsection, splitting through the left forearm as the gun fanned its third shot, punching through the arm and into the blonde-haired man's gut. The blonde-haired man wheeled, dropping to one knee in the mud, a trickle of blood from the left corner of his mouth as he heaved forward, Rourke's second shot impacting into Deke's chest as the single action in Deke's hand—thumb cocked—fired, the bullet spitting into the mud less than three feet in front of him.

Rourke fired the Detonics a third time, the 185-grain jacketed hollow point punching into Deke's head, almost dead square between the eyes. The head snapped back, the body lurched forward and sagged into the mud.

Rourke got to his feet, mud dripping from his shirt and Levis, the heavy rain now washing around him in a torrent. Natalie was beside him—he could feel her hands on his left arm. He walked forward, toward the body in the mud. Deke—Rourke edged the body over with the toe of his boot. The body rolled, the gunhand slapped into the mud, the revolver fell from it. The pansy-blue eyes were wide open, the head cracked up the forehead—the eyes were just staring though as the rain fell against them, and for a moment Rourke could do nothing but stare down into them himself. He had kept his promise to the woman with the dead infant.

Chapter Thirty-Four

Rourke sat behind the wheel of the pickup truck, the windows barely cracked open for air, the rain driving down with almost unbelievable force. Rain still dripped from his hair, and the girl beside him and Rubenstein on the far passenger side were wet as well. The brigand force would be moving out and now Rourke, Rubenstein and Natalie were a part of it. One of the brigand outriders had returned in the aftermath of the gunfight. The paramils were now closer than Rourke or any of the brigands had thought them to be, and it was imperative now that the brigands head to safety and put as much distance as possible between themselves and the paramils while they found a secure site for the battle lines to be drawn.

The brigand leader, Mike, had rejected Rourke's offer to stitch his lower lip and stem the flow of blood. Rourke had shrugged and turned and walked back into the truck. Rourke had watched then, as eventually some of Deke's comrades had dragged his body from the mud. He'd watched too, as the townspeople were released. Wet, dirty, bedraggled and terrified, they had slunk past the pickup truck, some turning and quickly eyeing Rourke, then all of them starting to run as they'd headed out of the circle of trucks—alive. But Rourke had wondered if they were really better off now—the new world that had taken shape after the night of the war was a violent one, and Rourke knew that many of them would not survive. Some would die because they could not cope with the violence, some would perhaps eventually revel in it and become brigands themselves. Silently, he'd wondered how his own wife and two children were faring—were they even still alive? He felt the pressure of Natalie's hand on his and stared out into the rain. . . .

By evening, the rain was still falling and the weather had turned cold. Twice during the afternoon, one of the massive fuel tanker trucks had stopped and some of the bikes had refueled. Rourke had counted one, possibly two trucks loaded with gasoline and at least three trucks loaded with Diesel, he guessed—enough to keep the brigand army rolling for prolonged periods away from the remains of civilization. During the middle of the afternoon, one of the few brigand outriders brave enough to keep to his bike in the driving rain had pulled alongside Rourke in the pickup truck and shouted up that Mike, the brigand leader, had changed his mind on the stitches. Rourke had pulled off along the shoulder and passed the bulk of the truck caravan and then pulled alongside Mike's truck. The caravan had stopped then and Rourke, using improvised materials, had stitched together the lip. There was no anesthesia available, and Mike just consumed more of the whiskey he had been drinking ever since the fight in order to control his pain. The inside of the eighteen-wheeler trailer was fitted with a collection of sofas and reclining chairs and beds—things obviously stolen from all the towns along their route. And the walls of the eighteen wheeler were lined with weapons as well. If the other trucks were anything like the one Mike occupied, Rourke decided, the brigand force would decidedly defeat the paramils when the eventual confrontation came.

Rourke had asked the woman attending Mike—apparently his wife or mistress—what was the convoy's destination, and she'd confided that it was a massive plateau some fifty or sixty miles further out into the desert, with one road leading up only, defendable against almost any size army without air support—or at least Mike believed that. As Rourke finished the stitching and told the woman how to make Mike more comfortable, then started to leave, the woman had stopped him, saying, "Hey—whatever your name is."

"John Rourke," he'd told her.

"Well—John Rourke—listen. You did my man a good turn so I'll do you one—there's a kind of rule around here—any snatch that ain't claimed at night is open property for anyone in the camp. So you or the little guy had better be sleepin' with that chick you brought in with you, or you're gonna have a fight on your hands. There's almost twice as many guys as there's women around for 'em. You get what I mean?"

Rourke nodded, asking, "How'd you get teamed up with Mike over there?" He looked over her shoulder and saw the brigand leader dozing now in an alcoholic stupor.

"They hit my town, two nights after the war—weren't many of 'em then. Killed my ma and pa and said he'd kill me if I didn't treat him good. So I treated him good—we're kinda attached now, see," the woman told him.

Rourke said, "Doesn't it bother you how you got that way?"

"He coulda killed me too, I figure—so I owe him something."

Rourke looked hard at the woman, saying, his voice a whisper, "Yeah—and you know what you owe him, too, I think—right at the back of your mind somewhere. One of those bayonets over there in his kidney. Think about it. How old are you, anyway?"

"Seventeen," she said.

"You look at yourself in a mirror lately?" Rourke turned and walked to the partially open back door of the truck. The rain was streaming in, the floor boards were wet. Rourke had jumped down to the mud and snapped his coat collar up, then started back to the truck.

The drive had gone on then, and now as they slowly pulled into a circle for the evening camp, the rain heavier even than during the day, Rourke stared out into the darkness beyond his headlights. It had been hard to judge the height of the plateau, but the crude road leading up to it had been steep and narrow, and if Mike's woman had been right, the brigand leader's estimate of the defensive posture he would now have hadn't been off. All that needed defending was the narrow road itself, and a half-dozen well-armed men could have held the road against twenty times that number of equally well-armed attackers.

Soon, lights could be seen burning in some of the eighteen-wheelers' trailers, while others from the brigand group were erecting a variety of lean-tos and shelters on the lee side of the trailers to get as much protection as possible from the rain.

"What do we do now?" Rubenstein asked.

"Well, we can't sleep and cook and everything inside the cab here," Rourke said. "You and I take some of those ground clothes we've been using and run a canopy out from the rear bed of the truck—we can sleep maybe in the truck bed. After we cover the bikes and everything it should be pretty dry back there." Then turning to the girl, Rourke said, "And you can keep an eye peeled while Rubenstein and I get the shelter up—huh? And stay dry."

"I can do my share of the work," she said angrily.

"I know you can," Rourke said softly. "But you're not going to." He piled out of the truck cab then and closed his leather jacket against the rain, his CAR-15 and Python still in the cab with the girl. The mud had washed off his clothes and boots from his previous sorties throughout the day into the driving rainstorm, and as he moved through the mud now beside the truck bed, he could feel his feet sinking into it, feel the rain soaking through his damp Levis and running down inside his collar.

Rubenstein was already freeing the extra tarps and ground clothes from the truck. Fighting the wind, it took Rourke and the younger man several minutes to set up the covered portion of the shelter, sticking out perhaps seven feet beyond the rear of the truck and on a level as high as the sides of the truck bed itself. Days earlier when Rourke had cut wood for their first fire after finding the truck and the provisions, he'd cut small saplings and trimmed them to use as tent poles if need be, and once the "roof" of the shelter was secured and one of the sides dropped against the driving rain, it was relatively simple for him and Rubenstein to complete the ground covering and then secure the opposite sides of the shelter.

Over the roar of the rain and the rumbling of the truck engines around them, Rourke shouted to Rubenstein, "Paul—get the stuff from the truck so we can get some food going. I'll get Natalie out." Then Rourke took one of the spare ground cloths and walked around through the rain to the front of the pickup, hammered on the window with his fist and signaled to the girl to open up. Using the ground cloth like an umbrella against the rain, he helped the girl from the truck, secured his weapons and made sure the truck was locked, then, with her huddled beside him, started back toward the impromptu tent.

Rubenstein had already broken out the small Coleman stove and the Coleman lantern and was sorting through the Mountain House meal packets. Natalie found some of the fresh water and put some on to warm up, then started making some order out of the chaos of the shelter.

They ate later in relative silence, all three exhausted from the ordeal of the day. At Rourke's suggestion, they broke out another botle of the whiskey and each drank, but only moderately. Finally, the shelter flap partially open for ventilation, as they sat beside its edge staring out into the rain, Rubenstein asked, "John—what are we gonna do now? It looks like they'll be setting up for a battle as soon as the rain slacks up."

Rourke sighed heavily, lighting one of his cigars and holding the flame of the Zippo for Natalie's cigarette. "The paramils won't be moving far in this weather—they looked less prepared for rough weather than the brigands did. I don't think we're gonna see much before this lets up, probably not for several hours afterwards. I could be wrong. I'd imagine if Mike's awake, he's putting out guards by that road, just in case. Depends on how tough the paramils are."

"We gonna try and get out?" Rubenstein asked.

"We can't," the girl said. "Not until the battle starts and if we're still up here, I don't see us getting out then."

"She's right," Rourke said. "Once the battle starts, depending on whether or not we're here, then we get out. But if we are still up here, that's going to be next to impossible. Just have to do our duty as good brigand troopers and hope the bad guys win instead of the good guys."

"The paramils are good guys?" Rubenstein asked, laughing.

"Well, I admit we had a kind of bad experience with them. But somebody's gotta go up against the brigands and it doesn't look like there's any kind of government left."

"What do you think *is* left?" Rubenstein queried,

taking off his glasses and rubbing his eyes.

"Probably more of Russia than there is of us," Rourke said, glancing toward the girl. "But I don't know for certain. Looks like a good deal of the country is going to be uninhabitable for a long time. Look at this weather we're having, too. It's supposed to be hot out there, but I bet the temperature is pushing down to forty or so. You notice the sunsets? Each night they've been a little redder. All that crap from the bomb blasts is getting up into the atmosphere and staying there."

"You mean we're all gonna die?"

As Rourke started to answer the younger man, the girl cut in, saying, "No—listen. Just trust me, because I know something about this. The radiation couldn't have done that much damage. The world is going to survive—I just know it."

Rourke looked at her, saying, "I know you know it—and it's not Natalie, is it? At least not in the language you grew up with. Right?"

Rubenstein started getting up, saying, "What do you mean—not in the language she grew up with? You mean she's . . ."

"Sit down and relax, Paul," Rourke commanded, his voice low.

The girl sighed heavily, snapping the butt of her cigarette through the opening in the shelter flap and into the mud outside. "He means I'm Russian."

"Russian!"

"She's one of the top women in the KGB—the Committee for State Security—the Russian version of the CIA and FBI rolled into one," Rourke said, exhaling a cloud of the gray cigar smoke.

"What—you!" and Rubenstein started toward her, but Rourke's left hand shot out, pushing against Rubenstein's chest and knocking the younger man back. Rourke glanced down. The medium-frame automatic size four-barreled COP derringer pistol was in her right hand.

Her voice was trembling as she rasped, "Please Paul—I don't want to use this, please?"

"What do you mean?" the younger man said. "You mean after all we've been through together, after the way you lied to us? We saved your life, lady!"

"I didn't ask you to come along and find me. I don't mean any harm to either of you—I almost love you both—please, Paul!"

Rubenstein was starting to get to his feet. Rourke—almost in one motion—pushed Rubenstein back and twisted the COP pistol out of the girl's hand, saying, "Now both of you—knock it off!"

"Knock it off?" Rubenstein demanded, his lips drawn back in a strange mixture of incredulity and anger. He pushed the glasses off the bridge of his nose, saying, "It's not enough that the Russians have destroyed the world practically, they killed millions of Americans—yeah, knock it off! What about you, John? You gonna knock it off? Just 'cause you miss your wife and you think maybe she's dead and this one comes along and she's a knockout and she's got the hots for you to get into her pants? What—you think I'm blind? She's a goddamned communist agent, John!" and Rubenstein was shouting.

"I didn't drop any bombs, I didn't give any attack orders, Paul! Leave me alone!" The girl nervously pulled another cigarette from the pack and tried lighting a match, but her hand was shaking so badly the matches kept breaking. Rourke took his lighter and flicked it, holding the flame for her.

She looked at him in the glow of the flame, saying, "Well—what are you going to say?"

Rourke leaned back, closing the lighter, saying, "He's right, you're right. You didn't drop any bombs—you were just being a patriotic Russian. And now you're here in this country and you're looking for Samuel Chambers. What? To kill him? So he doesn't serve as a rallying point for resistance? Right?"

"I'm just doing my damned job, John. It's my job!"

"I had a job like that once. But you know what I did? I quit. That's where you remembered me from—South America, a few years ago. I was down there a lot in those days. I didn't quit because my philosophy changed or anything—I just quit because I wanted to and figured I'd done my time. You could do the same, couldn't you?"

"I've got other reasons," she said, staring into the cigarette in her right hand. "I believe in what I'm doing."

"You didn't see your face when you looked at those refugees, the woman with the dead baby. You're on the wrong side."

"Is that why you didn't try and kill me when you recognized me?" she asked, looking up at Rourke.

"No—that isn't why," Rourke answered.

"How long have you known, John?" Rubenstein asked.

"Long enough—after the first couple of days I was

sure." Then turning to the girl, he said, "Is Karamatsov here too? You always worked with him down south."

The girl said nothing for a long moment, then, "Yes."

"Who the hell is Karamatsov?" Rubenstein said, leaning forward.

Rourke started to answer, but the girl cut him off, her voice suddenly lifeless-sounding, Rourke thought. "He's the best agent in the KGB—at least he thinks so and everyone tells him that. He's—I guess it doesn't matter—he's in charge of the newly formed American branch of the KGB—he's the top man in your entire country. The only man who can overrule him here is General Varakov—he's the military commander for the North American Army of Occupation."

"This is like some kind of a nightmare," Rubenstein started, taking off his glasses and staring out into the rain. "During World War II, my aunt was trapped over in Germany when the war broke out. They found out she was Jewish and they arrested her and we never heard from her again. I grew up hating the Nazis for what they'd done. What the hell do you think American kids are gonna grow up hating, Natalie? Huh? How many houses and apartment buildings and farms—schools, office buildings . . . how many places just stopped existing, how many children and women and little dogs and cats and everything else that matters in life did you people kill that night? Jees—you guys make Hitler look like some kinda bush leaguer!"

"This was a war, Paul," the woman said. "We had no choice. The U.S. ultimatum in Afghanistan, there was no choice, Paul—no choice. We had to strike first! And then your own president held back U.S. retaliation until the last possible minute—we didn't know!"

"Do you hear what you're both saying?" Rourke asked quietly. "Things haven't changed at all since the war, have they?" Rourke closed his eyes and leaned his head back against the edge of the pickup's tailgate. No one spoke for a while and all he could hear was the unseasonably heavy rain.

Chapter Thirty-Five

Rubenstein had elected to sleep in the bed of the pickup truck and was snoring occasionally as Rourke and Natalie lay beside one another under the tarps, listening to the rain. An hour earlier, one of the brigands had passed by, sticking his head under the shelter flap, then seeing Rourke and the girl together, grunted, "Sorry, man—I didn't know if—see ya," then walked away. Rourke had had one of the Detonics pistols under the blanket, the hammer cocked and the safety down, his finger against the trigger.

After the man had gone and Rourke had lowered the hammer on the pistol, the girl started to cry. Rourke heard the strange sound from her before he turned and saw the tears. Then he asked her why.

"He's right—what we did," she whispered, her voice catching in her throat.

"Yes, Paul is," Rourke said. "But if everybody who isn't Russian winds up hating everybody who is Russian, what's that gonna do, huh?"

"What kind of man are you—he was right, he was right, you know," the girl said to him. "I did try everything I could to get you to come after me—I guess I still am. What? Was it because you knew who I was, thought I was Karamatsov's woman or something?"

"That didn't really have anything to do with it," he said, then fell silent. The rain fell heavily and Rourke glanced at his Rolex—it was well after midnight. The girl spoke again.

"Why then?"

"Why then what?" Rourke said, not turning to look at her.

"What we were saying before—you didn't care that I was a Russian agent, that I might be Karamatsov's woman—then why?"

"Forget it," Rourke whispered. "You'll wake the kids," and he pointed up toward the truck bed, listening to Rubenstein snore.

"I won't forget it," she said. "Is it that wife you have—the one who's maybe still alive? What are you afraid of—you'll stop trying to find her?"

"No—I won't stop," he said. "Give me one of your cigarettes—I don't want to smell up the place."

The girl turned away from him a moment, fumbled in the pocket of her jacket and handed Rourke the half-empty pack. Then she took it back, extracted one of the cigarettes and lit it—her hands steady, the match lighting the first time. She inhaled hard, then passed the cigarette over to Rourke. He stayed on his back, the cigarette in his lips, staring up at the top of the shelter and the darkness there.

"Is it that you'd be unfaithful to her?" Natalie said,

her voice barely above a whisper.

"Somethin' like that," Rourke said, snapping ashes from the tip of the cigarette out the partially open flap and into the rain.

"But—what if she isn't—" and the girl left the question unfinished.

"Then it wouldn't be somethin' like that," Rourke said quietly, dragging hard on the cigarette, then tossing it out into the rain.

He could feel the girl moving beside him under the blanket. "Are you human?" she whispered.

He turned his head and looked at her, then without getting up reached out his left hand and knotted his fingers into the dark hair at the nape of her neck, drawing her face down to him, looking for her eyes by the dim light there through the shelter flap. All he could see was shadow. He could feel her breath against his face, hear her breathing, feel the pulse in her neck as he held her.

Her lips felt moist and warm against his cheek as she moved against him, and Rourke took her face in his hands and found her mouth in the darkness and kissed her, her breath hot now and almost something he could taste, sweet, the release of her body against him something he could feel in her as well as himself, She lay in his arms and he could hear her whispering, "You are human."

Rourke touched his lips to hers again, heard her say, "Nothing is going to happen, is it John?"

"I don't know—go to sleep, huh? At least for now," and he felt her head sink against his chest and heard her whisper something he couldn't hear.

Chapter Thirty-Six

Rourke opened his eyes, glancing down at the watch on his left wrist. It was three A.M. The girl was still sleeping in his arms, and to see the face of the Rolex he'd had to move her. He heard the sound again, a shot, then another and then a long series of shots—submachine gun fire, light like a 9mm should sound. "The damned fools," Rourke said aloud, feeling the girl stirring in his arms, then feeling her sit up beside him.

"Shots?"

Then Rourke heard Rubenstein, sliding off the pickup truck bed, beside them suddenly under the shelter. The rain was still pouring down outside, and Rourke stared out from the shelter flap, then pulled his head back inside, his face and hair wet. Without looking at either Rubenstein or the girl, Rourke said, "The damned fool paramils—it's a blasted night attack. Damn them!"

As Rourke pulled on his combat boots, whipped

the laces tight and tied them, the sound of the gunfire became more general, shouts sounding as well from all sections of the brigand camp, the engines of some of the big eighteen-wheelers roaring to life and, as each did, the shots were drowned out for a moment. Rourke shouted to Rubenstein, over the din, "Paul, start getting this shelter taken down and get the truck ready to roll—Natalie, give him a hand! I'm going up by the road." Rourke slipped into his leather jacket, got to his feet in a low crouch and started through the shelter flap, then dove back inside, shouting, "Mortars!"

He dove onto the girl and Rubenstein, knocking them to the shelter floor. The shelter trembled, the ground trembled, the blast of the mortar was deafening. Then came the sounds of rocks and dirt hitting the shelter, added now to the drumming of the rain. Rourke pushed himself up on his hands, rasped, "Hurry!" and started back toward the shelter flap, then into the rain. There was the whooshing sound of another mortar round, and though the pouring rain muffled the sound, he instinctively dove left, the mortar impacting behind him and to his right. Rourke pushed himself up out of the mud, the CAR-15 diagonally across his chest in a high port as he ran zigzag across the mud, avoiding the brigand men and women running everywhere around the camp in obvious confusion and panic. Some of the eighteen-wheelers were starting to move, inching forward, then backward, the very shape of the circle in which they'd parked prohibiting them from maneuvering. Some of them were entrenched deep in the mud of the plateau, and mud sprayed into the air as the wheels bit and slipped and dug themselves deeper.

Ahead of him, from the glare of the truck headlights and the few lanterns, Rourke could see a knot of several dozen men by the head of the single road leading up to the top of the plateau, and he could see the flashes of gunfire and hear more small calibre automatic weapons fire.

Rourke spotted Mike, the brigand leader, without a shirt, his body visibly trembling in the cold, the riot shotgun in his hands. As Rourke ran up to the men around Mike, the brigand leader stopped talking and glared at him a moment, then nodded slightly, and went on. The words were hard to make out with the missing teeth and the stitched, swollen lip. ". . . ey can't get up here after us. I figure maybe we got fifty or a hundred of 'em trapped halfway up the road down there in the dark—we keep shootin' into 'em, we're, ahh—we're gonna pin 'em down all night—first light we get we can finish 'em."

"What about the mortar rounds—all you need is one hittin' a fuel tanker and this whole spot is a huge fireball. I don't think that can wait till morning." Rourke heard some of the brigands grunting agreement, one from the rear of the knot of men around Mike shouting out, "One of them mortar rounds almost hit my truck—I was parked right next door to one of the diesel tankers. The new guy's right!"

"All right, smart ass," Mike said, turning to Rourke, "what do we do—huh?"

"You're the leader," Rourke said, hunching his shoulders against the rain. "But if I were you, I'd take about fifty or seventy-five men, maybe in two groups, and work my way down both sides of the road—right now. No shooting at all until you reached those fifty or so guys in the middle of the road. Try and get 'em by surprise, maybe, then from their position, you can just dig in and start pouring out a heavy enough volume of fire to push that mortar crew back out of range of the top of the plateau. If you dig yourselves in well, by the sides of the road rather than by the middle, you can keep your casualties down, then just before dawn, pull back. Hold your fire then until the mortar crew gives the middle of the road a good enough workout to figure you've pulled back, then start firing from the rims of the plateau here—you might even catch 'em out in the open trying to retake the position in the middle of the road. Simple."

Mike didn't say anything for a long minute, then, "You volunteering to lead one of the two groups?"

Rourke sighed heavily, then said, "Yeah—wait 'til I tell my lady what's up. You line up the guys—I'll meet you back here in five minutes." Without waiting for a comment, Rourke started in a slow run back across the camp and toward the pickup truck. He had no intention of sitting out the rest of the darkness in a foxhole in the middle of the road.

Another mortar hit off to Rourke's right as he took shelter beside one of the truck trailers, then he started running again—back toward the pickup truck. Natalie and Rubenstein—their differences, Rourke judged, put aside—were drenched, the girl's hair alternately plastered to her forehead or catching in a gust of wind, Rubenstein's glasses off and his thinning hair pushed back in dark streaks. The lean-to was down and Rubenstein was just closing up the gate of the truck bed.

"We gotta get out of here—fast," Rourke said, standing between them both. "I don't have any kind of good plan, but it's the best I can think of—now listen," and Rourke leaned forward, saying, "I'm leading a group of the brigands down along one side of the road, there'll be another group on the other side—kind of pincer-type thing. When we reach the paramils—there are maybe fifty of 'em in the middle of the road about halfway up to the summit—we're going to knock them out, then lay down some fire on that mortar crew to push 'em back out of range of the plateau. Before they hit one of the fuel tankers. Now," Rourke continued, "once I get down there and you hear the mortars stopping or pulling back, you and Paul take the bikes—"

"Wait a minute—shh, I hear something," the girl said.

Rubenstein looked skyward, saying, "Yeah—so do I, John. Listen."

Rourke looked skyward. He could see nothing but blackness, the rain still falling in sheets across his face and body and the ground on which he stood. "I hear it, too," Rourke almost whispered. "Helicopters—big ones and a lot of them—the paramils don't have that kind of equipment—"

Suddenly, the entire campsite, the whole upper surface of the plateau was bathed in powerful white light, and there was a voice, in labored English, coming over some kind of loudspeaker from the air above them. Rourke turned his eyes away from the sudden brightness. The voice was saying, "In the name of the Soviet People and the Soviet Army of Occupation you are ordered to cease all hostilities on the ground. You are outnumbered by an armed force vastly superior to you—lay down your arms and stay where you are."

Behind him, Rourke heard Paul Rubenstein, muttering, saying, "You can all go to hell!" And as Rourke started to turn, Rubenstein had the "Schmeisser" up and had started firing.

Rourke shouted, "Down!" and grabbed at Natalie, forcing her down into the mud, the roar of heavy machine gun fire belching out of the darkness above him, Rubenstein crumpling to the mud, doubled over, the SMG in his hands still firing as he went down. Rourke crawled across the mud toward the younger man, then the voice from the helicopters shouted over the speaker system again, "No one will move! Lay down your arms and surrender or you will be killed!"

Rubenstein's eyes were closed and Rourke could barely detect a pulse in the neck. Natalie was beside Rourke in the mud. As Rourke raised Rubenstein's head into his lap, he glared skyward. Still, he could see nothing but the light.

Chapter Thirty-Seven

Once Samuel Chambers' advisors had stopped arguing, one of the naval officers—second in command to the air force officer, the ranking military man—had suggested using a Harrier aircraft to travel to Galveston. It could fly low, below radar, was fast, armed, and could land or take off vertically, with the capability to hover, if necessary. Chambers had agreed. The flight from the Texas-Louisiana border area had been short and, Chambers admitted to himself, exciting. The Harrier accommodated only two men, himself and the pilot, and he felt happy that he wasn't too old yet to have been able to stare into the darkness and the rain they had encountered halfway through the trip and fantasize that he had been at the controls himself. He had flown twin engine conventional aircraft for many years, but never a jet. As the Harrier aircraft began to touch down in the Cemetery parking lot just outside Galveston, Chambers felt almost as if now he had flown a jet, and the feeling was good to him, uplifting, rejuvenating—better than the air of depression that he could feel settling over him when he thought of the sad state of affairs on the ground.

Because the plane had been for two men only, he was without his aide, without security. He had armed himself, borrowed a .45 automatic from one of the National Guardsmen, and the pilot was also armed, with a small submachine gun. As the plane touched down, any fears Chambers had held of security problems on the ground vanished. He could see more than a dozen men in U.S. military fatigues, holding M-16s and coming out of the shadows and toward the landing zone, itself illuminated with high-visibility strobe lights that had been placed there, Chambers understood, just for his arrival.

The aircraft slowed its engines and there was a loud whining noise as it stopped, the landing completed. The pilot scanned the ground, then made a thumbs-up gesture to Chambers behind him and the canopy over their heads started to open with a hydraulic-sounding hiss. The apparent commander of the soldiers on the ground stepped toward the plane, saluting, saying, "Mr. President—we've been waiting for you, sir."

The pilot stepped out and reached up from the wing surface and helped Chambers out of the co-pilot's seat in the camouflage-painted jet. Chambers climbed out over the side of the fuselage, awkwardly and conspicuously, he thought, then down onto the wing where the pilot helped him to the ground.

Chambers smiled at the army officer—a captain—and then turned to the pilot, extending his hand, saying, "Well, lieutenant—I enjoyed that flight. Got my mind off the troubles we all have for a few moments—it was like twelve hours' sleep and then a date with a pretty girl and a steak dinner all rolled into one!"

The pilot smiled, taking the offered hand, then his eyes hardened, his hand drew back and swept down to the small submachine gun slung diagonally across the front of his body. Chambers spun on his heel, as rough hands smashed him against the side of the aircraft fuselage, then a coughing sound, once, twice, and splotches of blood appeared almost magically on the pilot's forehead and he fell back against one of the wing flaps.

Chambers pushed himself away from the fuselage and started to run from the plane, away from the circle of lights. Looming up ahead of him were several men, all clad like those by the plane, in military fatigues. From behind him, he heard a voice, the English perfect, but odd-sounding when he heard the name the voice spoke. "I am Major Vladmir Karamatsov, Mr. President, of the Committee for State Security of the Soviet—you are under arrest. You are surrounded. You cannot escape. If you attempt to resist, you may only become unavoidably injured."

Chambers stopped running, his breathing hard. He smoked too much, he told himself. He wondered if getting to the pistol under his windbreaker would do any good.

"I assume, sir, you may be armed—I would advise against any attempt to use a weapon against yourself or any of my men. It would only result in needless bloodshed."

"Needless bloodshed?" Chambers shouted angrily. "What about that boy—the pilot? What about him—major?"

"He was armed with a submachine gun and would have used it—we were protecting your life as well. Since he likely had orders to prevent your falling into our hands."

"Bullshit!"

"Perhaps—but that is unimportant—now, your weapon. You will hand it over—please!"

Chambers surveyed the dark faces beyond the edge of the light, then shrugging his shoulders reached slowly under his windbreaker. He heard the sound of a rifle bolt, he thought, then heard Karamatsov shouting something in Russian. Chambers produced the gun and held it out from his body. The major was walking across the lighted area toward him, left hand extended, in the right hand a strange-looking handgun with a very long, awkward-looking barrel. The major was saying, "Please do not attempt any useless heroics, Mr. President. You can be of greater value to the American people alive rather than dead—we mean you no physical harm."

Chambers closed his eyes and felt the pistol being taken gently from his hand.

Chapter Thirty-Eight

The Soviet forces had landed two of their helicopters on the plateau, the others still hovering overhead, their floodlights illuminating the rain-soaked ground in a white glare that Rourke was almost getting used to as he knelt in the mud, using the pressure of his right hand to stem the bleeding from the gunshot wounds in Rubenstein's abdomen.

The girl had ignored the Soviet commander's directive to stay beside the vehicles and approached the nearest helicopter, shouting something in Russian which Rourke had been unable to catch with all the noise and confusion. He could hear gunfire from the ground level below the plateau and assumed the paramils were making a run for it, trying to use the darkness to hide their retreat. Rourke also assumed they were getting cut to pieces from the air.

The shirt Rourke was holding against Rubenstein's open wound was saturated with blood now and Rourke pulled his handkerchief from his pocket and placed it over the shirt to absorb more of the blood.

He looked down to Rubenstein's face—the younger man was pale, the circles under his eyes bluish in the harsh light. The pulse was weak and the breathing labored.

Rourke looked up as he heard boots sloshing across the mud toward him. It was Natalie, holding a Kalashnikov pattern assault rifle in her right hand, a Soviet officer and two enlisted men with her. She stopped, standing in front of Rourke where he knelt in the mud, holding Rubenstein. "John—I've identified myself to the commander—Captain Machenkov. I had to tell him both of you were my prisoners. But don't worry. I'll straighten everything out with Karamatsov. Paul will get the best medical care we can give him and you and Paul and I will be flown out of here in a few minutes to Galveston where we have a small base already operational. I know there's a field hospital there and between what you can do and our own doctors, I know Paul will be all right. Don't worry."

"What now?" Rourke said, looking up at her.

"I'm going to have to take your guns—the .45s. I told them you were my prisoners, but you have saved my life and because of the situation here on the ground I'd let you remain armed. It was the best thing I could think of—they don't speak English. This officer is a doctor."

Rourke glanced around the camp. Mentally and physically he shrugged, looking back up at Natalie, saying, "I can't move my right hand until we get a better bandage worked up for Paul—explain that to the doctor. If you need my guns now, you'll have to take them yourself."

"John—please don't try anything—I know you, remember. And I promised, everything will be all right. After Paul is well, you and Paul can leave—with your weapons and everything. I've even arranged for your motorcycles to be taken along."

"You really believe that?" Rourke said in a low whisper.

"Karamatsov is my husband, John—I really believe you'll go free. He'll do as I ask."

"Mrs. Karamatsov, huh? Any kids?"

"Don't be funny," she snapped. "No one knows about it—except for you, now."

With his left hand, Rourke opened his leather jacket, exposing one of the twin .45s under his arms. "Go ahead—without the right facilities, Paul's going to bleed to death. Go ahead—take them," and Rourke held open his coat. Natalie reached down, grasping one of his pistols, her face inches from his.

She whispered, "There wasn't any other way—believe me."

Rourke said nothing.

Chapter Thirty-Nine

Rourke ran his hands through his hair and stood under the steaming hot water. It was the first real shower he had had since the war had started and he was mildly surprised that he hadn't contracted head lice or something worse. He had washed his hair and his body at least four times and now stood under the steaming water, letting it work itself across his aching muscles and joints—he had been more tired than he had realized. Rubenstein was in surgery and Natalie had convinced Rourke that the doctors would do all they could. Rourke doubted little the efficacy of Russian medicine—they had pioneered a great deal since the close of World War II and he respected their methods. There was an armed guard standing outside the shower room, and after Rourke was finished and dressed, the next step would be actually meeting Karamatsov—and then the whole thing would start, Rourke knew. He closed his eyes and let the water splash across his face. . . .

Wearing clean clothes—they had been washed for

him—and his boots, he walked along the corridor between the four armed uniformed men toward the door at the far end. The complex was entirely underground, and Rourke supposed it had once been used by American forces. Above it was a small air base where the Soviet helicopter had landed. After Natalie had given some instructions to the KGB squad that had met them on the ground, Rubenstein had been whisked away by medics already waiting, and Rourke had been taken below then as well. He had been treated well, even given hot food—but all under the eye of armed guards. He assumed that by now Natalie had rejoined her husband—he had suspected the marriage—and Rourke also assumed that if the girl had been sincere in her promise, she had by now realized that it had been a promise she would be unable to keep.

No plan of escape had yet presented itself and Rourke realized he could do nothing really until Rubenstein's condition stabilized. He hoped he could stall until then, but he doubted it. Karamatsov would assume that he was still active with the CIA and act accordingly. Rourke absently wondered if, were the shoe on the other foot, he would do any differently.

The guards stopped, the lead man on the right knocking on the single light gray door. Rourke heard something in Russian, then the door opened. Karamatsov stood in the doorway. Rourke had seen the man before. He said, "Major—haven't seen you since Latin America—how many years ago?"

"John Rourke—the middle name is Thomas—you have a wife—"

Rourke interrupted. "Many men have wives, major." Rourke's eyes were smiling but his voice was level, even.

As if he hadn't taken note of Rourke's comment, Karamatsov continued, "Yes—a wife and two children—a boy and girl, if I remember your file correctly. I see you are still active in the Central Intelligence Agency."

"Where do you see that, major?"

"Let us talk inside." As the guards started into the office, Karamatsov waved them away, saying in Russian, "He cannot escape—wait at the end of the corridor." Then, turning to Rourke, he said in English, "You speak our language, don't you?"

"You know I do," Rourke said, his voice sounding tired to himself.

"Yes, I know—come in." And Karamatsov stepped aside and Rourke walked into the office. There was a dirty ring on the wall behind the desk at the far end of the long, low-ceilinged room—Rourke assumed there had been an air force or other military insignia on the wall, taken down after the neutron bombing of the area had killed most of the resistance and the Soviets had occupied the facility. As the helicopter carrying himself and Rubenstein and the girl had swept over Galveston coming into the base, the sun was already up, and Rourke had seen much of the real estate below them generally intact, but no signs of life, the trees and other plant life dead—even the grass brown and withered.

He saw Natalie sitting on a soft chair by the wall flanking Karamatsov's desk. She looked at him and smiled. Rourke sat down in the chair opposite Karamatsov's desk and waited, hearing the soft footsteps of the KGB officer coming across the carpet behind him, then seeing the major circling the desk. Karamatsov stood behind the desk for a moment, smiling, then sat down, saying, "So—I understand you saved Natalia's life—you and the injured one—Rubenstein. He's a Jew, isn't he?"

"I thought you were a communist, not a Nazi."

"We have found Jews to be troublemakers in the past—I was only curious. We as yet have located nothing about him in our data banks. He is new to your agency?"

Rourke started to answer, but Natalie cut him off. "Vladmir—stop it! I have told you—Rourke no longer works for the CIA and Rubenstein is just a magazine editor who fell in with John after their plane crashed."

"Then what about this?" and Karamatsov hammered his fist down on the desk, Rourke's identity card revealing the reserve connection with the CIA in his hand, the same card Rourke had shown on the airplane before he had taken over the controls after the pilots had been blinded the night of the war.

"You know they have a reserve list," the girl said.

"That is easy for you to say, Natalia—you are tired, this man saved your life, you have both undergone a great deal together. But I will handle this!"

Rourke reached across onto the end of Karamatsov's desk, opened a small wooden box there and saw cigars inside. He took one, unbidden, and then reached for the desk lighter. As Karamatsov reached toward his hand, Rourke eyed the man and Karamatsov drew his hand away. The KGB major said,

"You apparently were given to understand by Captain Tiemerovna that you would be released after the Jew was treated by our doctors. You will not be released, of course, as I'm sure you realized. But, you will have the opportunity of assuring your continued safety and good treatment, simply by telling us everything you know about the remaining strength of the CIA in your country, all that you have learned in your travels since the purported crashing of your commercial jet—everything. If you do this, you will remain alive and be treated fairly. Otherwise, I need not be specific. We are both men of the world."

Rourke studied the tip of his cigar, saying to Karamatsov, "No, I didn't believe her—but I'm glad she believed herself. I'm no longer in the CIA, haven't been for a long time. And if I were, I wouldn't tell you anything anyway—you want information, get out the guys with the pentathol and the hypos, then you can find out I don't know a damned thing. If you want to know what I saw after the plane crashed, I'll tell you—it's no military secret. Every town we passed was either abandoned or knocked off by the brigand gangs—like the people your troops grabbed back on the plateau when they picked us up. At least you guys did somethin' right."

"He's right," Natalie said, her voice sounding low and cold to Rourke.

"Then I will tell you some things, Rourke—your president committed—he is dead. You have a new president—Samuel Chambers. We captured him less than an hour before you arrived here. He is resting comfortably under guard in this same complex. I will give you time to rest as well—while the surgery is completed on your fellow agent. Then—"

"He is not my fellow agent," Rourke almost hissed, hammering his right fist down on the edge of Karamatsov's desk.

Karamatsov leaned back, a smile crossing his lips, saying, "Rourke—I remember when we met in Latin America. You were so confident, so good at what you did—even Natalia commented about it. I understand from what she has reported to me that your talents have remained undiminished. If you now show the intelligence you did then, you will make a decision—a decision for life, rather than death. Natalia tells me you still entertain the hopes that your wife and children survived the bombing. As well you should. I will propose to you something that you may wish to consider.

"If you show what you are really made of, if you are the man of wisdom Natalia has told me of," Karamatsov went on," you will not only survive—you can become one of us. We will help you to find your family if they still survive. You can have a position of prominence in the new order—"

Rourke interrupted him. "You sound like a Gestapo officer from *The Late Show* or something. Bite my ass."

Karamatsov stood, his face livid, his voice quaking with rage, "You speak to me this—"

Rourke, his voice barely above the level of a whisper, said, "I'd chew you up and spit you out if those guards weren't out there, Karamatsov. And I'll tell you this. You'd better make sure your people keep a good eye on me, or kill me right now, or you're gonna wind up with the prettiest widow in the

KGB." And Rourke glanced toward Natalie, watched her face, emotionless, watched her hands bunching into nervous-looking little fists.

Karamatsov pushed a buzzer on his desk and in seconds the door behind Rourke opened and Rourke could hear the guards coming. He didn't turn around. In Russian, Karamatsov, his voice still unsteady, rasped, "Take this man out and secure him in the rooms on the lower level—watch him!"

Rourke smiled, standing. He set the burning cigar down on the desk, stubbing it on the blotter and letting it lie there. "Get out," Karamatsov growled in English.

Chapter Forty

Captain Reed sucked on the empty pipe in his mouth, glanced one more time over the shoulder of the radio operator and turned on his heel and started through the doorway. He strode down the narrow basement hallway and up the stairs two at a time to the main floor of the house. He could hear through the open doors to the library the voice of Colonel Darlington, calm, collected, and the raving of Randan Soames, the paramilitary commander. Soames was shouting, "Over a hundred of my men were killed by them gawd-damned commie bastards, colonel—and you want me to calm down!"

Reed knocked on the door, then entered without waiting to be bidden to do so. Soames was starting to speak and Reed cut him off. "Colonel—I just checked down in the radio room personally. The frequency for the Harrier is open, and if Lieutenant Brennan were aboard, he'd be picking us up—I ordered a shutdown on that frequency. I figured the Russians could try and use it as long as we keep it open to get a fix on us. I think they got Brennan and captured the president."

Soames was still talking, as if, Reed thought, what he had just said had no meaning. "They got more than a hundred of my boys while they was attackin' this gang of renegades up on some damned plateau out there in the middle of the night in a gawd-damned rainstorm. Just come down in their helicopters nice as they pleased like they owned the whole damned place."

"They do, for now at least," Colonel Darlington said, knitting his fingers together and glancing to Reed.

Reed said to Soames, "Sir—haven't you heard what I said? I mean, the loss of your men is important, it's terrible—but they must have nailed President Chambers, when he landed in Galveston!"

"We can get a new president," Soames said quietly.

"No—we can get this one back," Darlington said. "I've been considering this, and I think Captain Reed and the others would agree with me. It's time we showed the Russians we can still fight. According to what's left of military intelligence in the Galveston area, the Russians have taken over one of our top secret air bases down there—I worked there for a time. The underground complex is hardened and would have protected anyone inside from a neutron air burst. They would have been trapped there until the Russians landed and by then it would have been too late. That air base is probably being used by the Russians right now—probably where they have Chambers. Probably got a couple hundred of our airmen imprisoned there too—wouldn't have had the time to get 'em out to a detention center, or the equipment free to do it with."

"You want to make a strike, sir?" Reed stuffed tobacco into his pipe and looked at Darlington.

"What do you think captain—your boys on the ground, some of my people in the air in some more of those Harriers—could we do it? Get in and get Chambers out, maybe free our boys—hurt the Russians a little and let 'em know we're still alive and kicking? Soames' men could back you up—he's got the numbers on his side there."

"We could land about seventy-five miles from there, then push in."

"Closer than that—I can get you within twenty miles of the base. You want to try it—they're your men. Reed?"

Reed looked at the air force colonel and nodded, striking a match to his pipe. Soames was still muttering about the "gawd-damned commies."

Chapter Forty-One

Rourke heard a knock on the door of the small two-bunk room he was locked in, then the door opened and Natalie was standing there. She was wearing a long-sleeved white blouse, a black pleated skirt and low-heeled shoes, her hair styled, make-up—it was hard for Rourke to remember the way she had looked back on the plateau—the mud stained jeans, the wet hair plastered to her face. And she hadn't looked vastly different, just drier, in Karamatsov's office—Rourke checked his watch—three hours earlier. "May I come in, John?" she asked.

"You run the place, I don't—come ahead," Rourke told her, standing up as she entered the room.

"I thought I'd let you know—they got Paul out of surgery and they're holding him in what you'd call intensive care—but he's fine. No major damage to the intestines or whatever—I don't know a lot about anatomy. They've got a tube in his stomach for drainage, but he's going to be all right."

"That's good," Rourke said, then, "Thanks—

look, I know you tried. I'm not angry at you, really—you did what you could."

She didn't say anything for a moment, then, "I saw Chambers—he's well. They haven't sedated him or anything. There's a plane coming from Chicago to pick you up—they'll want to take Chambers, too. General Varakov wants to see you both. Actually, you're lucky—Varakov is a good man. He'll be easier than Vladmir would have been."

"Yeah, real lucky," Rourke said, not trying to disguise the bitterness in his voice.

"I brought you a cigar," she said, her face brightening. She handed it to him, then reached into the right-hand pocket of her skirt and pulled out her cigarettes and a lighter. She lit the cigar for Rourke, then her own cigarette. She sat down beside him on the bed. "John?"

"What?"

"You aren't in the CIA anymore, are you?"

"I told you I wasn't—all I'm interested in for now is finding my wife and children."

"Tell me about them, John—all of them."

"Why?"

"Just tell me about them, please," she said, her voice a whisper. Rourke stared at her, watched the deep blue eyes, the exquisite profile.

He dragged on the cigar, saying, "Well, my son Michael is six—smart, independent little guy, but what do you say—he's a neat little man. There's Annie—my daughter, she's just four—kind of funny, cracks you up sometimes, pretty like her mother. And sometimes she drives you crazy."

"What's your wife like?" Natalie asked.

"Sarah—dark hair, brown though, not like yours. Gray-green eyes, about five-seven. She's smarter than I am. She's more—what would I say—she's more of a diversified person, wider interests—she's—"

"Do you love her that much?"

"We talked about that already, didn't we?"

"Give me an honest answer to one question," the girl said.

"All right, if I can," Rourke told her, watching the tip of his cigar, not wanting to look at Natalie.

"If you'd never met Sarah, didn't have Michael and Ann—would you have—ahh—never mind, John," and she started to stand up.

Rourke put his left hand on her forearm, his hand moving down to her hand. "Maybe I'm crazy," he said, forcing a smile.

"No," she said quietly. She looked at the door, then hitched up the skirt over her right leg and Rourke saw the COP pistol, the little stainless steel .357 Magnum, strapped to her right thigh with a length of white surgical elastic. She undid the elastic, stuffing it under the pillow on the cot, and weighed the gun in her hand, then pointed it at him.

"John—your weapons, Rubenstein's weapons, they're in my husband's office. He's learned of an attack on the base—here, late tonight. We have a spy in Chamber's organization in east Texas. Vladmir is calling down a neutron strike at the time the attack starts, then you and Chambers will be flown to Chicago. You'd never find your wife and children. Rubenstein would be made to talk, when they found out he didn't know anything, they'd kill him then. You wouldn't leave here without Chambers, would you?"

"Honest?" Rourke asked, looking into her eyes.

"I know you wouldn't. If I help you—to get Paul out and Chambers too, would you promise me one thing—that you wouldn't kill anyone you didn't have to?"

"Yeah—I'd promise that," Rourke answered.

"And that includes Vladmir—that you wouldn't kill him—only if you had to, to defend yourself?"

"Do you love him?" Rourke asked her.

"I don't know," she said flatly. "Get ready—I'll get the guard in here."

She stood up and walked to the door, smoothed her hair back from her face and tapped on the door, saying in Russian, "Corporal—come in here. This prisoner had a weapon—I've disarmed him. Come inside immediately and assist me."

The door opened, the young corporal said, "I will assist you, comrade captain," then stepped through the doorway. As he passed her, the COP pistol clamped in her right fist, she straight-armed him in the right side of the neck. Rourke stepped forward and caught the young soldier before he hit the floor, then eased him onto the bed. As Rourke stripped the man's weapon away, then used the military trouser belt to tie the man, the girl stood by the door, watching. Rourke, over his shoulder, said to her, "How are you going to get out of this?"

"Don't worry about me. We can get Chambers freed, then get Paul out. I have already arranged for your motorcycles and equipment to be brought to one of the elevators they use for getting the planes up onto the field. There's a prop plane down there—it's fueled and flight checked. You can fly it?"

"Unless the gauges are in Arabic, I'll do okay. Why are you doing this?"

She looked at him, saying, "I gave my word—I keep my word, just like you do."

He didn't say anything to her as he checked the young unconscious guard's AK-47, but he could see her smiling.

Chapter Forty-Two

The girl behind him, Rourke edged along the wall toward the base of the stairs. The hall there was in shadow, light streaming from the head of the stairs above on the main level of the underground complex. Chambers was being held just beyond the head of the stairs, with two security guards outside his door and a third inside with him as a suicide watch. On this same floor, one level below the ground-level runways and the few ground-level hangars, was the hospital wing and Karamatsov's office. Rourke had explained to Natalie that he had to confront her husband, had to stop Karamatsov from calling in the neutron strike against the attacking forces. Once he was airborne with Chambers, he'd try every frequency he could to contact the U.S. forces on the ground and alert them that the attack could be called off because Chambers was free—that would be Rourke's end of the bargain with Natalie for his freedom.

He glanced up the stairwell, saw the booted feet of

a guard and pulled his head back, using hand signals to warn the girl beside him. She moved up to the base of the stairs, smoothed her blouse and palmed the COP pistol in her right hand, behind her skirt, then started up the stairs. Rourke held back at the edge of the stairwell, not daring to look up lest he give the girl away. He heard bits and pieces of a brief conversation in Russian, then a shuffling of boots and a heavy thudding sound. He raced around the corner of the stairwell and halfway up the stairs intercepted the body of the Russian guard, rolling down toward him. He dragged the man down the stairwell, took the AK-47 and as he started to tie the man, stopped, realizing the guard's neck was broken and he was dead.

Rourke started up the stairs. Natalie was standing three stairs down, looking along the corridor. Rourke stopped a stair below her, saying, "He's dead—you do it?"

Her face was expressionless, then the corners of her mouth turned down and she said, "I had to—he realized something was wrong."

"At least he was right about that," Rourke said, glancing back down the stairs. "Where are they holding Chambers—along there?"

"Around the corner," Natalie whispered. "Come on." Rourke had no plan, other than to overpower the guards outside the door if Natalie couldn't connive her way inside. It was the guard on the inside that he was worried about—he judged that the man on the suicide watch was also on a death watch, ordered to kill Chambers if it appeared he was being rescued.

Rourke flattened himself below the top stairs, watching from the floor level as Natalie walked down the hallway and turned the corner. Rourke saw no one, heard nothing, pushed himself up and started across the hall, along the near wall, waiting at the corner, listening to the sounds of Natalie's shoes down the corridor. There was—again—a conversation in Russian. He could make out enough to realize she was having some difficulty convincing the guards she should be allowed access. Finally, he heard her say, "Would you care for me to leave, then come back with Comrade Major Karamatsov? Must he inform you personally that I am to see the prisoner to secure an important item of information—immediately? Well—what is it?" and Rourke could hear the sound of her footsteps coming back along the hall toward him, then the heavier sound of one of the soldier's boots against the floor, the man's gruff-sounding voice, the grammar so bad even Rourke could recognize it as bad, saying, "Wait, Comrade Captain Tiemerovna—you may of course see the prisoner, Chambers. We were only trying to do—"

"I know—and you should be commended for it—but there is no time. Hurry," and he could hear footsteps going away from him, "Hurry, there is no time—open the door!" Rourke heard the door open, then turned into the hallway and started for the two soldiers in a dead run, hoping to get the drop on the two men. Halfway down the length of the hall, he knew it was no good. One of the guards was already turning toward him. Rourke's finger edged inside the trigger guard of the AK-47 and squeezed, his first three-shot burst cutting into the nearer guard. He heard an isolated shot then, heavy-sounding, like a big bore pistol. He dismissed it from his mind, firing another three-round burst into the second guard as the man reached for the alarm buzzer on the door frame. The guard collapsed against the wall, his hand grasping toward the button. Rourke ran up beside him, knocking the hand aside with the butt of the AK, then kicking open the door into Chambers' room.

Natalie was standing inside. A third Russian guard lay on the floor, dead, a neat hole in the middle of his forehead.

The graying, tall man Rourke recognized from news footage as Samuel Chambers was staring at Natalie, then turned, looked at Rourke and said, "You the Marines?"

"No, Mr. President," Rourke said, letting out a long sigh. "Just a talented amateur. Are you all right?"

"I am for now."

Rourke turned back into the hallway, snatching up the two AK-47s from the fallen guards and passing one in to Chambers, then giving the second gun, plus the spare AK he already carried, to Natalie. She slung one across her back, checking the magazine on the one in her hands. Rourke looked at her, saying, "I'm sorry—I tried not to have to do that."

"I know," she said quietly. "Come on—we have to get Paul."

"Who's this Paul?" Chambers asked.

Rourke started to answer, but the girl cut him off, saying, "Never mind, Mr. President—once you meet Paul you'll love him."

Rourke just looked at her, saying, "You and the president get Paul—unless you think you'll need me. I've gotta stop Vladmir—more than ever now since the shooting started. Where's that elevator?"

"At the end of the corridor along here," she said, "then make a hard right and take it all the way to the end. You'll start seeing the aircraft maintenance area before you get there—but hurry. Every guard will be turned out."

Rourke stepped back into the hall, snatching two spare magazines from one of the fallen guards, then starting back along the hall toward the far end where Karamatsov's office was. When he was only halfway along the corridor's length, he could hear a siren starting. Three uniformed Russian soldiers suddenly appeared from a doorway, one of them carrying his AK-47 in his right hand, the others with their weapons slung across their backs. Rourke opened up with the AK-47 in his hands, catching the first guard before he even looked up, then firing short bursts into the other two as they made for their weapons.

Rourke continued down the hallway, reached Karamatsov's door and stepped back from it, firing a three-round burst into the lock and ducking aside as the door swung open. There was a burst of automatic weapons fire from inside the office.

Rourke flattened himself along the wall, shouting, "I don't want to kill you, Karamatsov, unless I have to—listen to me."

There was another burst. Rourke stared back down the hallway. In minutes or less, he realized, the halls would be swarming with Soviet soldiers, and all would be lost. Rourke dumped the nearly spent magazine from the AK-47 and slapped in a fresh one, then, extending his right arm on line with the open door into Karamatsov's office, he fired, angling the muzzle up and down, right and left, in short bursts. Then Rourke dove through the doorway, rolling across the carpet. Karamatsov was up, firing from behind the desk, and Rourke loosed a burst just above the desk, as Karamatsov ducked down.

Rourke was on his feet, running, then he jumped across the desk as Karamatsov raised himself to fire. Rourke's hands reached for the KGB major's throat, his right knee smashing upward into Karamatsov's groin, both men falling to the floor behind the desk. Rourke had a plan now, and his promise to Natalie aside, he couldn't kill Karamatsov—the Russian was the only ticket down the corridor and to the aircraft elevator with Chambers, Rubenstein and the girl.

Karamatsov wrestled Rourke's hands away from his throat, a small revolver appearing in his right hand. Rourke wheeled, smashing the knife edge of his left hand into the inside of Karamatsov's right wrist, punching the gun out of line with his own body and onto the floor. Rourke crossed his body with his right fist, lacing against Karamatsov's jaw, knocking the Russian back against the wall, then diving to the floor for the revolver. Automatically, as his right hand reached for the gun, Rourke started to roll, a desk chair crashing down onto the floor where his head had been a second earlier. The revolver was in Rourke's right fist now and he extended his arm, his thumb cocking the hammer as his arm straightened, the muzzle of the little blue Chief's Special .38 on line with Karamatsov's face. The Russian froze.

"You so much as blink, you're a dead man," Rourke said, his voice barely audible. He got to his feet and moved toward the Russian, spinning him around against the wall, doing a fast light frisk, keeping the muzzle of the little revolver against Karamatsov's right temple. Rourke glanced over his shoulder. There were four Russian soldiers crowding the doorway. Rourke shouted, "Move and Karamatsov gets it," in Russian, then saying, "I mean it!"

Rourke punched the muzzle of the revolver against Karamatsov's temple, rasping in English, "Tell them—now!"

In Russian, the voice edged and trembling with rage, Karamatsov commanded, "Do as this man tells you—that is my order."

"Wonderful," Rourke whispered to Karamatsov. "Now—tell them to get out of here and clear the corridor. In about two minutes you and I are walking out of here and the first man I see with a gun means you're a dead man—got me?"

Karamatsov said nothing, then Rourke pushed the muzzle of the revolver harder against the KGB man's head, repeating, "Got me?"

"Yes—yes—I understand." Then, in Russian, Karamatsov repeated Rourke's instructions. One of the soldiers started to say something and Rourke increased the pressure of the little Smith & Wesson's muzzle against Karamatsov's temple, and Karamatsov shouted something Rourke didn't quite understand, but the soldier fell silent and all four men left.

"You're being real good, Vladmir—I'm proud of you," Rourke said softly, the gun still at the

Russian's head. "Now—where are my guns—be quick about it!"

"In the closet," Karamatsov said.

"Fine, let's go get them." Rourke walked Karamatsov toward the closet, never moving the revolver's muzzle from the man's head. Karamatsov opened the closet and Rourke had him reach down the twin .45s, the Python and the two-inch Lawman from the closet shelf, then had him take the CAR-15 and the Steyr from the corner of the closet. "Where's the bag with the magazines and ammo?"

"I don't know—I think with your motorcycles."

"Good," Rourke almost whispered. "Now, on your knees, and real careful, check out each one of those pistols and the CAR-15 so I can see they're loaded—hurry it up!"

As Karamatsov knelt and one by one inspected the weapons, slowly so Rourke could see that they were loaded, Rourke slipped the shoulder holster in place, switching the Chief's Special at Karamatsov's temple from one hand to the other as he secured the stainless Detonics pistols under his arms, then got Karamatsov up off the floor.

"Now—hand me that belt with the Python on it," Rourke said. Rourke slung the belt on his left shoulder, moving the muzzle of the Metalifed six-inch .357 to Karamatsov's head and tossing the little Chief's Special into his hip pocket. Rourke slung the CAR-15 to his right shoulder—he'd had Karamatsov chamber a round—then flicked off the safety. He slipped the two-inch Lawman into his belt.

"Forgot my knife—where is it?" Rourke asked.

"In my desk," Karamatsov said.

"Let's go get it—and my wallet and lighter, hmm?"

Never moving the muzzle of the Python from Karamatsov's head, Rourke walked slowly beside the Russian to the desk. The Russian started to open the top drawer and Rourke pushed him away, then opened the drawer himself. There was his wallet, and the black chrome Sting IA and his Zippo—and a Pachmayr-gripped Model 59 Smith & Wesson 9mm automatic. "I would have killed you, Vladmir. Hey—what do people call you for short—Vladey? I like that—I'll call you Vladey," Rourke said, smiling. "Now Vladey, we're gonna walk down that hallway, you're gonna carry my Steyr in that nice padded rifle case—be real careful with it. Fantastic gun—come up my neck of the woods sometime and I'll show it to you. Great shooter. Now, you carry it, walk real slow and don't try to get so you can't feel this—" and Rourke gestured with the muzzle of the Metalifed Python—"against your head. 'Cause if you stop feeling it there, I'll pull the trigger." Rourke thumb-cocked the hammer on the Python, his first finger against the grooved trigger. "All right—let's go."

Karamatsov didn't move, saying, "Kill me now."

Natalie was blown, she would be fingered for helping him escape, Rourke knew that, and he said, "I promised your wife I wouldn't unless I had to—your choice. You want to be a dead hero, or you want to live again to fight another day—which is it?"

The Russian started walking toward his office door. Rourke switched the Python into his left hand, his right fist wrapped around the pistol grip of the

CAR-15, his finger against the trigger. They entered the corridor and Rourke spotted at least a dozen Russian soldiers halfway along its length. "Shout to them," Rourke whispered.

In Russian, Karamatsov almost screamed, "I gave an order—it is to be obeyed—let us pass and stay out of sight. That is my order!"

The soldiers, some slowly, vanished from the corridor. Rourke started walking faster, saying to the KGB man, "Let's pick up the pace a little—I'm runnin' a little late. Where's the radio room?" Karamatsov said nothing for a moment, then Rourke repeated the question. "Where's the radio room, Vladmir? Hmm?" and Rourke punched the muzzle of the Python harder against the back of Karamatsov's head.

"By the aircraft maintenance section—at the far end of the corridor and to the right. But you'll never make it."

Rourke pushed a little harder with the muzzle of the Python, "You better hope I do, pal—it's us, remember. I don't make it, you don't make it. Move."

Rourke started walking faster, Karamatsov just ahead of him. They were halfway down the corridor, and ahead of him, Rourke could see more of the Russian soldiers, and as he started to say something to Karamatsov, the Russian shouted, "Get away from here! That is an order!"

"Good," Rourke whispered, glancing around the hallway. There was no one behind him, but he knew that as soon as they reached the end of the hall and turned right, the corridor would fill with Russian soldiers, just waiting for their move.

"What do you want in the radio room?"

"You're going to call off the air strike with the neutron device," Rourke told him.

Karamatsov stopped, not moving. "She told you that?"

"I'm a psychic," Rourke said. "Now move unless you want your brains decorating the ceiling tiles—come on."

Karamatsov started walking again, saying to Rourke, "Why would I call off the air strike, and even if I did, why would they listen to me?"

"You'd better hope they do," Rourke said. "Because when I get out of here—with Chambers—I'm going to try and save your tails and get the assault force called back, if I can. We're in the same spot, friend. 'Cause I'm leaving here through the elevators onto the air field, and if I'm reading this place right, this wouldn't be a neutron hard site with the access doors open to the elevators—so all you guys would get fried. You tell your bosses that," Rourke concluded. He knew nothing about the construction of the underground complex and had no reason to suppose that the site would be vulnerable with the access doors to the elevator section opened, but he was gambling that Karamatsov and his superiors wouldn't be sure of that, either.

They reached the end of the corridor and turned right. Behind him, Rourke could hear the shuffling of boots, but there was no one ahead of him. "How far's the radio room, Vladmir?"

"There," and the Russian raised his hand, slowly, gesturing toward a door perhaps a hundred yards down. "That is it."

"Good," Rourke said. "Now, when we get there,

you knock on the door and they bring the radio microphone out to you—got it? We don't go in." Rourke could see the KGB man's shoulders sag slightly. "And when it comes up, they can use alligator clips to make the connection if the microphone cord's too short."

The Russian started to turn his head and Rourke gave the Python a little nudge and the movement stopped. "You will never make it out of here alive, and if by some chance you do and you do not kill me, I will find you, if I have to search this entire dung pile of a country. I will look and look until I find you."

"Because of this," Rourke said, nudging the gun slightly, "or because of her?"

"What do you think?" the Russian snapped.

"Nothing happened—it could have, but nothing did. I think all you've got is a very lonely girl. You were already married to your job when you married her. It happens to a lot of guys in a lot more prosaic jobs. She's a hell of a good woman—you're lucky. I guess that's maybe the real reason I don't want to kill you."

Karamatsov stopped and turned, ignoring the muzzle of the gun at his head, staring at Rourke. Rourke whispered, "I almost envy you—with her. If you're fool enough to lose her, I should shoot you," and Rourke pushed the muzzle of the Python against Karamatsov's head again and they walked the last few yards to the door of the radio room. "Now knock—be polite," Rourke whispered.

Karamatsov knocked on the door, shouting in Russian, "It is Major Karamatsov—open the door—immediately."

The door opened and there was a soldier there with

a gun in his hand and Rourke, in Russian, said, "Put it away or you've got a dead major—you want to be responsible, go ahead and be a hero of the Soviet Union." The soldier hesitated a moment, then stepped back into the room. "Call for the radio hookup," Rourke rasped to Karamatsov in English.

The Russian hesitated, then shouted into the radio room. In a moment, the same young Russian who had appeared at the door with a rifle appeared with the microphone, passing it to Karamatsov. Rourke jockeyed Karamatsov into position, so he could see the inside of the radio room over the Russian's shoulder. He glanced down the hallway, saw a face peering around the corridor, then the face withdrew. Rourke said to the KGB man, "Now, get on the radio and make it good—call off the neutron strike. Remember, my Russian's just fine."

Karamatsov pushed the button on the microphone and began speaking into it, then from the speaker inside there was heavy static, then a guttural voice, coming back to him. Rourke listened to the voice on the speaker and Karamatsov arguing, Karamatsov finally admitting the situation he was in. There was a long silence, then the voice was replaced by another voice, speaking in English.

"This is General Varakov—your name is Rourke, no? I do not want Karamatsov killed, at least not yet. He was too proud, perhaps this will be good for his—what is it—the Latin word, the ego. Yes. I have called off the neutron weapon strike. I will meet you some day. It is hard for me to believe you are acting alone, though."

Karamatsov glanced toward Rourke, and for a

moment Rourke could read his eyes, then Rourke took the microphone from Karamatsov, saying, "General—I wasn't acting alone. I freed President Chambers and he helped me—you've got a tough adversary in him. I'll give you some advice—don't underestimate him."

"And some of the advice for you, my young friend," the voice on the loudspeaker came back. "You have just used all the nine lives of a cat this night. Do tell this to your President Chambers—do not underestimate me." And the radio went dead.

Rourke ripped the microphone free of the cord and tossed it down the empty corridor, saying to Karamatsov, "Now let's get out of here so I can call off the attack before it gets started." Running in a slow lope beside the KGB man, the gun still trained on the Russian's head, Rourke started down the hallway toward the aircraft maintenance section. Behind him, he could hear the shuffling of the Russian boots on the corridor floor, but he didn't bother to turn around.

Chapter Forty-Three

The elevator section of the underground hangar and maintenance complex was huge, more vast in size than Rourke had ever imagined. The twin engine prop plane was ready, the bikes loaded aboard, Chambers—Rourke had breathed a sigh of relief finding that the new president knew how to fly—was at the copilot's controls. At gunpoint, Natalie had moved Rubenstein, complete with the I.V. and the stomach tube, from the hospital section, and had him already loaded aboard. She had said nothing to her husband as Rourke had brought Karamatsov in still at gunpoint. The doors leading to the elevator section were closed behind them, massive steel doors that effectively sealed the compound.

"How are the RPMs, Mr. President?" Rourke shouted in through the hatch in the port side of the fuselage. The president gave a thumbs-up signal and Rourke turned back to Karamatsov, saying, "Well, major—looks like we take off. Do I have to cold cock you—that's slang for knock you out—or will you just stay here and wait?"

Karamatsov said nothing, then Natalie spoke. "I will guard him, John—you don't need to knock him out."

Rourke looked at her, saying, "I can't leave you here—you'll be—"

"If I go with you, I am still a KGB agent. Your people won't welcome me with open arms. Besides—" and she left the word hanging.

"I can let you off between here and there," Rourke suggested, his voice low.

"If the entrance doors are opened, they will be able to scramble some of the captured American fighter planes and pursue you—they'll shoot you down."

"I can't let you stay here," Rourke said. "What about what you've done?"

The girl looked at her husband, saying to Rourke, "I don't think Vladmir will admit to what I've done—he'll find a way to cover it up. Varakov doesn't want him dead, and Varakov would not kill me and leave Vladmir alive. Perhaps I'll just retire as an agent."

Karamatsov spoke, saying to Rourke, "I will not kill her."

Natalie cut in, saying, "No—he'll let me live. He'll remind me of it each time I look at him, with everything he doesn't say. Vladmir and I have been comrades together much longer than we have been husband and wife—I know his secrets, too."

"We've wound up in the middle of a soap opera, haven't we," Rourke said, smiling at the girl.

There was confusion in Karamatsov's eyes, and the

girl laughed then, saying, "That was a class at the Chicago school you did not have to take Vladmir, darling. The female agents were briefed on the story lines of the dramatic programs shown on television here during the afternoons—so we could convince another American woman that we were just like they were." Then she turned to Rourke, saying, "Does your Sarah watch these soap operas, John—or did she?"

"No," Rourke said, smiling at the girl.

"I didn't think she would," Natalie laughed.

Rourke reached into his hip pocket and handed her husband's revolver, the Chief's Special he'd pocketed earlier. He wanted to say that he hoped he'd see her again, he wanted to kiss her good-bye, but he stuck out his right hand, saying, "Good-bye?"

The woman smiled, the corners of her mouth raised slightly, her lips parted, and she leaned toward him and kissed him on his lips, almost whispering, *"Dasvidanya."*

"Yeah," Rourke said, stepping into the plane. "Hit the button for the elevator then and *dasvidanya*." Rourke started forward to the cockpit, and as he strapped himself into the pilot's seat and put on the headphones he thought of the woman—*dasvidanya* was like the German *auf wiedersehen*, he recalled. "'Til we meet again."

The elevator was rising, the doors above them parting, and through the open cockpit wing window Rourke could smell the night air. Rourke glanced over his shoulder at the sedated Rubenstein, sleeping a few feet behind them.

"Mr. President," Rourke began. "I may have to

pull up quick, so be ready to help me on the controls." Rourke reached over his head, checked the switches, and as the elevator stopped, hit the throttle, the plane starting forward into the darkness and across the runway. Rourke turned into the wind and throttled up, the runway fence coming up as they cut across the tarmac.

The president was shouting, "What are you doing?"

"I'm avoiding the trap they've probably got at the end of the runway—pull up now!"

And Rourke hauled back on the controls, the nose coming up, the plane bouncing against the runway surface, then lifting off, the fence clearing just below the landing gear.

Rourke left his running lights off, banking steeply, his right hand twirling the radio frequency dial. Chambers said, "Who are you calling on the radio, Mr. Rourke?"

"I made a promise, Mr. President—I figure if you get on that frequency they'll call off the attack for you."

"Why should I?" the voice asked out of the darkness.

Quietly, Rourke said, "Mr. President—with all due respect, this plane flies two ways—away from the Russians back there and right back toward them—don't think I wouldn't!"

There was silence, then Rourke found the frequency, hearing the ground chatter in English. "You're on, sir," Rourke whispered in the darkness.

He let out his breath when he heard the president begin to speak into the headset microphone.

Chapter Forty-Four

Rourke knelt on the ground, listening, the CAR-15 in his hands, the leather jacket zipped high against the night cold. He could hear dogs howling in the night, and throughout the late afternoon and early evening before dusk he had seen signs of trucks and motorcycles and men on foot in the woods and the dirt roads cutting through the forested areas. "Brigands here, too?" he wondered. He knew the ground he was covering—he had owned it before the night of the war and supposed he still did if anyone owned anything anymore.

He listened to the night for a moment.

After the flight out of the KGB stronghold, Chambers, by radio, had cancelled the night attack, but the attack had merely been postponed. There were several hundred airmen held prisoner at the base, the ground commander, an army National Guard captain named Reed had explained. Rourke wondered if by now, a week later, the attack had taken place. It was hard getting used to a world without news, without information. He had landed the aircraft in east Texas, where Rubenstein had been given additional medical aid and pronounced fit enough for limited travel less than twenty-four hours ago—Rourke checked the luminous face of the Rolex on his wrist. It was past eight o'clock, if eight o'clock indeed existed, he reminded himself.

Chambers, the air force colonel, Darlington, and some of the others had asked him to stay and fight with them, or work as their spy. They'd told Rourke that he would now be a hunted man, followed by the KGB, his name and face known. He'd told them he knew that already and that he had business of his own. And he was here now, at the farm. In the distance beyond the stand of trees, he would see the house, he knew, but he sat on his haunches by a dogwood tree—it hadn't bloomed for a long time, or at least when he had been there to see it. But he remembered it.

Intelligence reports had come in that Karamatsov had left the KGB base, and there had been a dark-haired, beautiful woman with him. Another report had indicated that Karamatsov had possibly been spotted by one of the growing network of U.S. operatives outside of the area immediately surrounding Texas and western Louisiana. There weren't enough reports yet to provide a continuous flow of accurate or even reasonably accurate information, but there were enough to provide interesting bits and pieces of information—and perhaps it was valid.

Rourke had left Rubenstein with one of the bikes and the bulk of the supplies about fifty miles southeast of the retreat. To have traveled on with the rough going of the last miles would have lost Rourke another twelve hours, perhaps, and the younger man had insisted he'd be all right until Rourke returned. Rourke had left him the Steyr-Mannlicher SSG, in a secure position in a high rock outcropping from which to shoot if necessary. Then Rourke had started toward the farm.

He had argued with himself silently all the long walk after he'd left his Harley hidden two miles or so back. He had tried to imagine a scenario for all the possibilities of what might have happened at the farm. In each case, he had determined that Sarah, Michael and Ann would no longer be there. But perhaps there would be a clue to where they had gone. There had been one scenario that he had rejected since the night of the war—that he would find their bodies there.

He was armed to find them, if they lived. The retreat contained more than enough supplies for several years, enough ammunition for his needs, and there was hydroelectric power, which he had engineered himself, using the natural underground stream as the source. The one thing he had lacked was gasoline and now he had that—by way of repayment, President Chambers had shown him a map, which afterwards Rourke had memorized and burned but was still able to reproduce from memory. It showed strategic reserves of gasoline cached throughout the southeast. For Rourke's comparatively meager needs, the supply was infinite.

Rubenstein had spoken of going south to Florida to see if somehow his parents had survived, and Rourke supposed that soon the younger man would.

He hoped Paul would return. Rourke had counted on few people as friends in life and Rubenstein was one of these few, perhaps the only one left alive. He supposed that perhaps he should count the Russian girl, Natalia—he rolled the name off his tongue in the darkness so that only he could hear it—had there been anyone else present.

After leaving Chambers, Rourke had used the twin engine plane to carry him across the Mississippi with the still weakened Rubenstein. There had been nothing. Once thriving cities were obliterated, the course of the river itself even seemed altered. From the air, Rourke had seen no signs of life, and the vegetation that still had stood had appeared to be dead or dying. Captain Reed had rigged the plane with a device similar to a Geiger counter that was a sensor which worked from outside of the craft. The radiation levels—if the device had been accurate—were unbelievably high.

Rourke had landed the plane just inside the Georgia line—what had been the Georgia line before, just below Chattanooga. The city was no longer really there—a neutron bomb site, Rourke decided, since the majority of the buildings were standing but there were no people at all.

Finally, the cigar burnt out in the left corner of his mouth, Rourke rose to his feet and started forward through the woods again, in a low crouch, a round already chambered in the CAR-15, the two Detonics .45s cocked and locked in the Alessi shoulder rig, the Python riding in the Ranger scabbard on his right hip. He had no pack, just a canteen and one packet of the freeze-dried food and a flashlight.

He edged to the boundary of the tree line and stopped. The frame of the house was partially standing, like bleached bones of a dead thing, the walls burned and the house itself gone. Rourke stood to his full height, the CAR-15 in his right hand by the carrying handle, awkward that way for his large hands with the scope attached.

He walked forward, hearing the howling of the dogs. The moon was full and he could see clearly, not a cloud in the sky, the stars like a billion jewels in the velvet blanket of the sky.

He stopped by where the porch had been. Michael had liked to climb over the railing and Rourke had always told the boy to be careful. Annie had driven her tricycle into the railing once, and knocked loose one of the finials, if that was what you called them, he thought. He remembered Sarah standing in the front door that morning after he had come back. She had taken him inside, they had had coffee, talked—she had shown him the drawings for her latest book, then they had gone upstairs to their room and made love. The room was gone, the bed, porch—probably even the coffee pot, Rourke thought.

The barn was still standing, the fire that had gutted the house apparently not having spread. He started toward the barn, then turned back toward the house, studying it for a pattern. After circling it completely, he had found two things—first, that the house had exploded, and second, the charred and twisted frame of Annie's tricycle.

Rourke sat down on the ground and stared up at the stars, again wondering if there could be places where the things that called themselves intelligent life had elected to keep life rather than wantonly spoil it. He looked at the wreckage of the house behind him and thought not. He started toward the barn, then stopped, hearing something behind him.

Rourke wheeled and dropped to his right knee, the CAR-15 thrusting outward. Four men, wild-looking, unshaven, hair long, clothes torn, started toward him, one with a club, another with a knife almost as long as a sword, the third carrying a rock and the fourth man with a gun. They were screaming something he couldn't understand and Rourke fired at them, the one with the rock going down, then the man with the club. Then he fired at the man brandishing the knife, missing the man as he lunged toward him. Rourke rolled onto his back, snatching one of the stainless Detonics pistols into his right hand, the CAR-15 on the ground a yard away from him. As the man with the knife charged at him again, Rourke fired once, then once more.

There was still the fourth of the wildmen, the man with the gun, and Rourke spun into a crouch, his eyes scanning the darkness. He heard a scream, like an animal dying, then fell to the ground, rolled and came up on his knees, the Detonics in both his fists, firing as the fourth man stormed toward him. The man's body lurched backwards and into the dirt. Rourke got to his feet and walked toward the man. He was really little more than a boy, Rourke realized. The beard was long in spots, but sparse, the hairline bowed still, the face underneath the beard looking to be a mass of acne-like sores. Rourke reached down for the gun—it was a reflex action with him, he realized. The pistol was old, European, and so battered and rusted that for a moment he couldn't identify it. The weight was wrong and he pointed the pistol to the ground and snapped the trigger. There was a clicking sound and Rourke looked up into the darkness and let the gun fall to the ground from his hand.

After a while, he reholstered his pistol and found the rifle on the ground. There was no thought of burying the four dead men, he realized. If he were to bury the dead, where would he start?

Mechanically, still half staring at the gutted frame of the house where his family had lived, he reloaded the Detonics and the CAR-15 with fresh magazines. He started away from the house, then turned, remembering he'd been walking to the barn before the attack. He opened the barn door—an owl fluttered in the darkness, the sound of the wings were too large for a bat. Rourke lit one of the anglehead flashlights that he and Rubenstein had stolen that first night in Albuquerque.

He scanned the barn floor—the horses were gone, but he had expected that. But so was the tack. He started toward the stalls, then remembered to flash the light behind him. He saw something catching the light, and he walked toward the barn door, then swung the door outward into the light of the stars and the moon.

It was a plastic sandwich bag, the kind Sarah had used for lunches she'd stashed in the pocket of his jacket when he'd left early in the mornings to go deer hunting. There was something inside it and he ripped the bag from the nail attaching it to the barn door. It was a check, the first two letters of the word "Void" written across it—it was Sarah's writing. He turned the check over, shining the light on it, and read:

> My Dearest John, You were right. I don't know if you're still alive. I'm telling myself and the children that you survived. We are fine. The chickens died overnight, but I don't think it was radiation. No one is sick. The Jenkins family came by and we're heading toward the mountains with them. You can find us from the retreat. I'm telling myself that you will find us. Maybe it will take a long time, but we won't give up hope. Don't you. The children love you. Annie has been good. Michael is more of a little man than we'd thought. Some thieves came by and Michael saved my life. We weren't hurt. Hurry. Always, Sarah.

At the bottom, the letters larger, scrawled quickly, Rourke thought, was written:

I love you, John.

Rourke leaned back against the barn door, rereading the note, and when he was through, rereading it again.

He didn't look at his watch, but when finally he looked up, the moon seemed higher.

He folded the half-voided check carefully and placed it in his wallet, looked up at the stars, and his voice, barely a whisper, said, "Thank you."

John Rourke slung the CAR-15 under his right shoulder and started walking, away from the barn, past the gutted house and into the woods. He stopped and looked back once, lighting a cigar, then turned and didn't look back again.